S0-CFC-020

No Place to Hide

No Place to Hide

by
Dorothy Martin

MOODY PRESS
CHICAGO

©1971 by
THE MOODY BIBLE INSTITUTE
OF CHICAGO
Paperback Edition 1975

ISBN: 0-8024-5939-0
Library of Congress Catalog Card Number: 73-163444

7 8 9 10 11 12 Printing/LC/Year 87 86 85 84 83 82

PRINTED IN THE UNITED STATES OF AMERICA

ONE

ALTHOUGH GRETCHEN didn't realize it at the time, it was David's discovery of the church that began the chilling nightmare that came so near to ending in tragedy. It was not until long after, when each separate event fell in place with terrifying clarity, that she saw the connection. But first came the phone calls, with heavy breathing the only response to her repeated "Hello?"; the stealthy movement of someone in the bushes outside the house and the sound of hands whispering along the window screen seeking entrance; the direct attempt on her life. It was a long time before she was able to sleep through a night without starting up and clutching at David.

If he hadn't found the church that Sunday morning, none of the terror would have happened. He would have laughed off the persistent remarks of old Mr. Adams as he pushed his broom around the office and talked about everyone needing to know God and be saved. If David hadn't walked past the church and stopped to listen, their lives would not have been touched by the evil of distorted minds. But whenever Gretchen thought of that later, she remembered that if David had stayed home that Sunday morning or gone his usual route to the drugstore, none of the rest would have happened either. And she knew in her heart that that would have been worse.

It was a warm summer morning after a leisurely Sunday breakfast that David crumpled his napkin beside his plate, stretched lazily, and said, "Guess I'll go for the paper."

Gretchen smiled back at him over the rim of her coffee cup. "I think we've hit that rut Aunt Phyl always was so contemptuous of in marriage. Though how *she* knew—"

"It's always the unmarried aunt who knows best how to raise the kids," he quipped back.

"Anyway, I didn't know you fell into the rut in such an ordinary way," she went on. "Every Sunday for the last three months you've said, 'Guess I'll go for the paper' as though you'd come to some dramatic decision."

"Listen, woman. When you spend five days a week making dramatic decisions, you just naturally go on making them the other two days."

"Like 'Shall I go for the paper before breakfast or after breakfast?' That's why you don't have it delivered, I'll bet, because then you wouldn't have that important issue to decide."

David shoved back his chair and stood up. "The real reason is it gives me a chance to get out from under your thumb." He smiled at her and pulled her up from the chair, holding her close and rubbing his cheek against her black hair.

Gretchen leaned against him and thought, *Poor Aunt Phyl*, and smiled at the incongruity of standing in the security of David's arms and thinking of Aunt Phyl who had hated men.

"What are you smiling about?" he asked, his chin bumping against the top of her head, and she pulled away enough to look up at him in surprise.

"How did you know I was?"

"Simple. I felt your cheek muscles move against my shirt. Since there's nothing for you to cry about —being lucky enough to be married to me—you could only be smi—"

Gretchen pulled away. "Look! Go get that paper and stop bragging on yourself."

"Walk with me?" he invited.

"Umm—" She considered it and then shook her head. "I'll put a pie in the oven while you're gone, and then I can read the paper while it bakes."

The kitchen was roomy but so efficiently spaced that it required little moving from refrigerator to sink to stove. Gretchen's deft fingers, sure from practice, made the pie crust and fitted it into the pan, sliced peaches and poured sugar and cream over them in the shell, and slipped the pan into the oven. The actions brought back memories of Aunt Phyl who had grudgingly taught her to cook.

She ran water into the sink to wash the breakfast and baking dishes, staring unseeing out the window, knowing that the line of zinnias marching the length of the garage and turning to cross the back of the yard made bright splashes of color against the green ground cover. But she was not consciously aware of them just then. Instead, she was back in thought in the apartment complex, seeing again their four rooms,

7

exactly like the other apartments—efficient, cramped, institutional. The smell of cabbage cooking next door or hamburger frying up the flight of stairs was an ever-present reminder of the seldom-seen neighbors—neighbors hardly worthwhile getting to know since they changed so frequently.

This, she remembered, was Aunt Phyl's world when Gretchen, deserted by parents who had tired of responsibility, had come into it. She'd been thirteen then and timid. And awkward and skinny. Now she had only bleak memories of the barren years that took her through high school. Not unhappy memories, just dreary. Aunt Phyl had worked long hours in an office, and she could feel again the silence of the rooms that she had come home to each afternoon from school. It had seemed impossible to make friends in the huge city school into which she had transferred in the middle of the year, so she had kept to herself, lonely in school and lonely in the apartment. She could never accuse Aunt Phyl of being consciously unkind. Gretchen knew now that Aunt Phyl's nature had been so introspective and embittered that she could give nothing to a questioning, longing-to-be-loved teenager who was there from necessity rather than choice.

As her hands automatically washed and put the dishes away, she remembered the endless weekends she had filled by learning to cook and sew and by reading books she had checked out of the library by the armfuls. By carefully saving everything she could from summer jobs, she had gone to junior college after high school graduation. Then Aunt Phyl had died.

Even now she could feel the shock of the moment when she had come out on a Saturday morning to see Aunt Phyl slumped at the kitchen table, an untasted cup of coffee in front of her. Though there had been no closeness between them, they had been together; and now again she was alone. She had finished out the month left of the second year of college and then had looked for a job. It was her knowledge of words learned through reading and her accuracy of spelling and punctuation that had gotten her the job in the publishing company where David worked.

The thought of him curved a quick smile on her lips and brought her back to the present. The magic of David in eight months of marriage had begun to wipe out the fears and insecurities that had shadowed her growing years. She turned to hang up the dish towel and stopped motionless, staring at the clock over the refrigerator. David had been gone forty-five minutes! For a three-block walk to the drugstore! She looked around her uncertainly. She could imagine that the clock was wrong, except that the dishes were done and the pie just ready to come out of the oven.

With a frown beginning to line between her eyes, she went through the living room, pushed open the screen door, and leaned out to look down the street. There was the usual Sunday neighborhood activity of lawn mowing, sunbathing, and across-the-yard visiting. Two houses away, Jack was cutting the grass, with Brian toddling after him, leaning down to pick up handfuls of grass and toppling over each time. Usually his bottom-heavy antics were amusing, but now she saw him with only partial recognition.

9

She looked anxiously down the street for David's tall, lean figure, but he was nowhere in sight. She looked back at Jack, debating whether to go over and say something to him. But how could you say to a neighbor, "My husband went out an hour ago to buy a paper and hasn't come home yet"? Especially to a policeman. It sounded too much like stories in the newspaper, only they weren't funny. They always turned out to be cases of desertion—

Gretchen turned from the door abruptly and sat down on the edge of the couch in front of the window, pulling the curtain just enough apart so that she could look out without being seen. As she watched the street, she listened unwillingly to the questions her mind whispered.

What did she know about David really? Would living with a person for eight months guarantee that the marriage would last forever?

She saw him now as she had that day she had gone to his office with a manuscript to be left for his final approval. He had looked up at her, his dark eyes direct, with a half-laughing, half-annoyed, "So you're the one who got saddled with this job. After you've been here a while, you'll know which ones to turn down."

She could still remember her surprise that she, green and inexperienced as she was, needing a job so desperately, might have a choice of which manuscripts she would read. It had shown in her expression, and he had shaken his head sternly.

"A lot of this is garbage not fit to print, let alone read. Be choosy or you'll be in muck all the time

—unless you like this kind of stuff.'' The last words were abrupt, and he had looked at her sharply. She remembered yet how she had shaken her head, her cheeks flaming at the memory of some of the scenes pictured and the words used in the manuscripts.

From that casual meeting a friendship had grown, and Gretchen had discovered a glow she hadn't known she possessed. It was David's doing, for he had looked beneath the outer shell of independence to the shy uncertainties it covered. He had brought her laughter and joy, and the shadows of Aunt Phyl's gloom had begun to fade. A year later they were married. Gretchen knew that David was from a small town in Iowa, that his one sister was married and had a large family, that one brother, much older than he, was dead, that his parents were elderly and unable to come for the wedding, though his mother had written her a warm letter of welcome, that he was a graduate of the University of Iowa with a major in journalism, that he had a quick sense of humor, that he was kind, steady, gentle, dear—

But now at this moment of panic, as the word *desertion* hung in her thoughts, she wondered if she *really* knew him. She only knew what he had chosen to tell her. He could well be tired of her by now. It had happened to her before.

Then another thought possessed her, and she jumped up to stand nervously at the door again, sure now that he had been hit by a car and had been taken to a hospital. There would have been no identification on him because he usually just stuck a handful of change in his pocket and left his wallet on the chest of drawers. No one would know who he was and would have no way of knowing whom to notify.

She pushed the screen door open again and stepped out into the sunshine that didn't warm her. Would Jack know if a person were found and taken to a hospital? How much longer should she wait before asking for help? She looked back at the living room clock—after twelve already!

Then she saw him striding up the street and, as he saw her, his smile flashed and he lifted his hand in the familiar wave, the newspaper stuck jauntily under his arm. The relief that washed over her was part anger and part release from fear.

"David! Where were you?"

"At church," he grinned back, letting the screen slam behind him.

Anger was uppermost then and she lashed out, "Don't try to be funny! I've been sitting here imagining you'd been hit by a car—or—" Suddenly she burst into tears, and David dropped the paper on the sofa and put his arms around her.

"Honey, I'm sorry! I wasn't noticing the time. You know I wouldn't have worried you on purpose."

"But where were you?" she asked again, her voice muffled against his shoulder.

"Just where I said—at church."

"There isn't a church anywhere around here." She stood back to look up at him accusingly.

"Well, not a church building. But there's a nursery school over on Lincoln Drive, and it's used on Sunday as a church."

"How did you know about it?"

"I've passed it a few times. Once several weeks ago I decided to walk to the drugstore a different way. When I came back and turned onto Lincoln, I heard people singing and found it was coming from this building. So I stopped to listen for a few minutes. Today I got interested and forgot the time and stayed until the end."

"Did you go in? In those clothes? With your stubble?"

He grinned back. "No, I sat outside. There are benches around the playground area, so I just sat down near an open window and pretended to read the paper—and listened."

Gretchen looked at him, curious about his interest. Religion was something they had never discussed. Not even when they planned their wedding had there been any thought of having it in a church. Since she had never gone to church, it had not occurred to her that David might have, or might want to. Since their first date, Sundays had always been their day, kept for themselves and not shared with anyone.

She thought back to his amusement several months ago when he had brought home the booklet someone had left on his desk. It had turned out that old Mr. Adams, the recently hired cleaning man had put it there. And, because David had been courteous and thanked him, it had encouraged the old man to talk further.

When he had told her some of the things Mr. Adams said, she had asked curiously, "Did you go to church? Before we met, I mean?"

He had shaken his head. "Not since I was a little kid

13

and went to Sunday school a couple of years. Oh, I went a few times to the campus church." He had shrugged. "All the chaplain ever talked about was being kind to your neighbor. Since I didn't plan to beat up anybody or cheat some widow, I figured there was no sense in giving up a morning of sleep to listen to that."

She wondered now as she looked up at his contrite face whether his interest in church now was being sparked by Mr. Adams' persistence. She asked, "Is Mr. Religion still talking to you?"

He nodded. "Still at it." Then he took hold of her shoulders to look down at her. His face was sober as he said, "Gretchen, I am sorry. I should have known you'd worry when a five-minute walk to the drugstore became an hour-long absence."

"I was just afraid you'd—been hurt—or something had happened," she stammered, not quite meeting his eyes for fear he would guess what other thoughts she had had. He knew, of course, about her parents, and she couldn't, she couldn't hurt him by letting him know she'd been afraid of the same kind of treatment from him.

The incident would have made an amusing story, told lightly and with just the right amount of exaggeration, but Gretchen didn't mention it later in the week when she picked up Ruth to go shopping. She wouldn't hint to anyone that she had a doubt about David. It didn't matter what she didn't know about him, she thought, as she pressed the horn lightly and waited for Ruth. His openness and transparency left no place for deceit. It was a facet of his character that had attracted her in the first place because it was such a contrast to her own instinctive reserve.

She smiled as she watched Ruth come toward the car, slowed to a crawl by Brian's chubby figure, adorable in his pantsuit with its mound of diapers bulging.

"What's so funny?" Ruth asked as she scooted Brian across the seat and slid in after him.

"Hi, sweetie," Gretchen said to Brian, but remembering David's comment last week that Ruth didn't look well, her eyes noted with concern the thin figure and the dark smudges under her eyes. She smoked constantly, of course, but she claimed she always had, and she dismissed cancer statistics with an impatient half shrug and a contemptuous twist of her lips.

Ruth hadn't waited for an answer but went on, "You're a *darling* to take me shopping at the last minute after I turned you down yesterday when I was so *sure* Jack was going to have today off because he's *supposed* to. But that's the trouble with the boys in blue, they can *never* count on anything, or rather their wives can't, even though the top brass talks all the time about 'our great police force' and how proud they are of 'each man who is so devoted to duty and serving mankind!' But what good does that do the wives and kids if they never know when *their* boy in blue is coming home—or *if* he's coming home?"

Gretchen was so used to Ruth's nonstop talking that she generally listened only enough to make the right comment to keep the monologue going. But this time the bitterness and shading of fear in Ruth's voice kept her concentrating on it all.

15

"Being a policeman isn't easy—" she began in sympathy.

But Ruth cut her off with a derisive, "Easy! It's murder!"

"Mommy cry." Brian, standing between them, leaned over to pat his mother's face.

Gretchen looked over at her quickly, and Ruth caught the glance and laughed raggedly.

"No, not now. Not that I couldn't at the drop of anything, but the baby is talking about this morning, poor lamb, when I was so mad at Jack for going to work when I'd counted on his being home and us just being together that I could have thrown something at him. But of course I didn't because it wouldn't have helped anyway, and of course it isn't his fault when they call him up and tell him all leaves and all days off have been canceled and to get over on the double. So this time Brian was my victim and had to stand around while I bawled my head off after Jack left."

Gretchen frowned. "I guess I only half listened to the news this morning. Was there something special—"

Ruth nodded. "This kidnapping over in that new section at the edge of town, or anyway they suppose it's a kidnapping because nobody has seen the little—" She stopped, glanced at Brian, and went on, "—the little b-o-y since early yesterday afternoon. They've got practically the whole force out looking for him, plus everybody in the neighborhood, and it isn't that I don't want him found or begrudge the help for the poor family, because I know how I would feel if—if—" She stopped, fighting tears, and finished with a burst of words, "It's just that it's *always* this way, and everybody thinks the police are wonderful when they happen to need them, but other times they don't think they're human or have feelings."

"People don't really think—"

"Yeah?" Ruth jeered. "You been reading the newspapers lately? You see who gets the stones and bottles thrown at them? The criminals? The kooks? No, the *police*. And when they try to protect other people's property and keep store windows from being broken and stuff looted, or even try to protect themselves, what happens? *They* get the blame, and they get threatened, and their families get threatened, and they get calls saying their kids will be—will be—" She broke off and reached to pull Brian onto her lap, hugging him so hard he squirmed.

Gretchen pulled into the parking lot and stopped the car, turning to face Ruth with worried eyes. "Has that really happened?"

Ruth nodded. "Jack got a phone call last week —only a crank call, he said and tried to pass it off." She looked down at her clenched hands. "The only thing is, I heard it on the extension, but Jack doesn't know that. And I'm scared."

That Ruth could speak so briefly and decisively made Gretchen realize how serious she was. "Someone just pulled a name out of the phone book," she said, trying to sound reassuring. "There must be a lot of sick minds who would think something like that was funny but wouldn't really mean anything by it or do anything."

Ruth looked away and said stubbornly, "All I know

17

is that Jack got a threatening phone call. And I'm afraid." She fumbled for the door handle. "Let's go. I hate to spend the money anyway, so let's get it over with."

Gretchen followed silently, seeing again the sharpness of Ruth's bones and the trembling of her hands as she reached to help Brian into the grocery cart. Maybe what she had always taken to be Ruth's quickness of motion was actually nervous tension. She felt guilty now for having given Ruth only superficial friendship in the five months they had been neighbors. When David had hinted that Ruth needed friendship, she had insisted that neighborliness didn't come easily to her. It needed more than a casual wanting to help to overcome the barriers of her natural reticence and the many years of hurrying past closed apartment doors to shut her own behind her. And anyway, she hadn't wanted to make any close friendships, hadn't needed any companionship apart from David.

Jack and Ruth hadn't forced their friendship. But they had invited Gretchen and David over for a backyard supper the evening they had moved in, and Ruth had come over to help hang curtains and wash the wedding dishes Gretchen had unpacked and put carefully on the shelves. Brian had been the bridge between them. Gretchen thought he was adorable and never could resist the arms he raised so trustingly to her to be picked up.

Ruth had said frankly when they first met, "You're so striking with your black hair and blue eyes that if I weren't sure Jack loved me I'd bare my teeth and show my claws every time you came around. And anyway," she had finished as Gretchen had laughed in embarrassment, "I can tell by the look in your eyes that you're crazy about your husband, so I guess Jack's safe."

Jack was so unlike David that Gretchen couldn't believe the comradeship that had sprung up between them. David was quiet, thoughtful, with a dry humor that caught one off guard and sometimes was too subtle to be understood by the casual listener. Jack was big and bluff and blond, his good-natured face weathered by exposure to the sun and wind as he walked his beat or took a turn in traffic. He was open with his own feelings and needs, and quick to sense and want to share someone else's burdens.

"That's why the bum is a policeman," Ruth said once, looking at him with her heart in her eyes. "He seems to think he was made to be everybody's guardian angel, when all I ask is that he look after me and Brian."

Jack was quick to splash beer in a guest's glass, but he was quick also to detect when it was not wanted and kept soft drinks in the house for David and Gretchen.

"Though there's nothing like a glass of beer to relax a guy and make him willing to open up. Nothing stronger, you understand. None of this getting drunk business. I've seen too much of it, especially when someone gets wrapped around a tree because of it. Homes are wrecked too." He shook his head while Ruth nodded agreement. "But like anything else, a little beer at the right time does a lot of good. Like I say, it relaxes you."

19

But David's quiet "No, thanks" at the first offer was respected, and no questions were asked. Only to Gretchen had he ever told the horror of the memories of the death of his only brother, an alcoholic. She could still hear the somberness of his voice when he said, "I used to take an occasional drink before that, but not after. Never after."

Her mind was busy with these thoughts as she filled her cart and then stood in line to be checked out and waited for Ruth. She couldn't get her mind off Ruth's outburst after she had dropped them off at home, helping Brian up the walk and into the house while Ruth carried in the groceries. It had taken longer to shop than she had planned on, and she had time only for a piece of fruit before going downtown for a noon dental appointment.

The light turned red as she came to an intersection and she stopped, her eyes on the light but her thoughts on Ruth. As she waited for the signal to change, she gradually became conscious of the throbbing sound of the car that had stopped beside her in the left-turn lane. Without thinking, she turned her head and half glanced at the convertible. The glimpse she had of the couple in it made her look away quickly. They were so obviously, passionately necking, so oblivious to their surroundings, that it was obscene. What should be a private, personal, loving thing was revolting, done as they were doing it, so openly in public. She had only a momentary glimpse of them, but it was enough to stamp on her mind the image of grubby blue jeans and matching shirts with wide cowboy belts slung low.

They should be wearing cowboy boots instead of going barefoot, one part of her mind observed absently. She was vaguely aware from her peripheral vision of the dark red splotches on the girl's arm nearest her. She sensed too that the girl had turned to look in her direction, but she kept her own eyes straight ahead while the light changed from red to green arrow for the left turn and finally to green. The convertible didn't turn left but shot ahead, cutting in front of her, and she had only a glimpse of the cardboard box on the back seat with the jumble of blankets and towels and bathing suits and other odds and ends.

She wondered if their mothers knew where they were and what they were doing. She wondered, too, what she and David would do if they raised a daughter—or son—for whom love meant sex. Which was worse? she wondered. To have the anguish of parents whose child had been kidnapped and was possibly dead—cut off with no chance of growing up—or the anguish of parents whose children grew up to drugs and illicit sex.

She pulled to a stop in front of the dentist's office and sat in the car, frowning. Then she shook herself from the morbid thoughts. It didn't have to be either/or. Even with her background, she had turned out all right. And so had David.

The thoughts returned to trouble her that evening, though, when the news was flashed that the little boy had been found murdered, his body partially buried in a shallow grave in a forest preserve. There were no clues as to who had taken him or why, since the

21

family had no money and there seemed to be no reason for the kidnapping. The police even declined to speculate if it were a so-called thrill killing.

Gretchen looked at the television pictures of the weeping parents; the worried neighbors as they stood in small knots, avid for details and clutching their own small children; the blanket that had been found on a trail in the woods; the shot of the sunny clearing in the forest preserve where the body had been found. She hoped Ruth was not seeing the pictures, but she knew she was. She knew, too, that Brian would have cause to pat her face and say his bewildered, "Mommy cry."

She thought later that it must have been these anxieties and uncertainties that made her willing to go to church with David on Sunday. He broached the subject Saturday evening as he reflectively wiped at a glass.

"You know, the neighbors around that place are going to call the police one of these days when they see me skulking around the nursery school. It would be kind of embarrassing if they did and Jack answered the call."

She laughed. "Well, why don't you go inside? As long as you're there, you might as well."

"Oh, I don't know—"

She looked at him as he left the sentence dangling. "What's the matter? You really are at church anyway if you sit outside through the whole thing."

"I know. But if I go in, then I'm with the people and I have to introduce myself—" He shrugged and left the sentence unfinished again.

"You're not bashful, are you?" she teased.

"Sometimes. But I wouldn't be if you were along," he coaxed. As she started to protest, he added quickly, "You don't want people thinking I'm a bachelor, do you?"

She was silent, knowing that she had no reason for not going, except that she just didn't want to.

"Do you *have* to go again?" she asked finally in a small voice.

He picked up a plate and wiped at it without looking at her. Then he said, "Mr. Adams has been bringing me more paper—booklets—to read. Most of it I just shove in my desk drawer. But now and then some of it—makes sense. I mean, it sounds reasonable, not the wild-eyed, haranguing stuff people hand out sometimes. And, from what little I've heard, this minister says a lot of the same things. In a different way, of course." He stopped, still wiping at the plate, and after a moment went on, "I keep thinking, what if we are missing something—something we need—"

"I'm not! I've got all I want. You. I don't need anything else."

" 'I have need of nothing'!"

He looked back at the questioning look she turned on him and gave her a puzzled frown. "Sorry, darling, a line from something, some book or other. And it seemed to fit."

"David, you know I *had* to learn to do for myself, not to count on anyone for anything until you. And I'll admit I need you. But you're different. You're real —not imaginary—ethereal—something dreamed up."

23

"But if I were to—"

She turned on him fiercely. "Don't say it!" Her voice was sharp with fright. "And even so—even if you did—no god, real or imagined, could take your place."

She turned and clung to him, and he put his arm around her comfortingly.

"Don't cry. Don't worry. I'm sorry I upset you." After a moment he said with a chuckle. "Let's just say I want to see what the minister looks like. I think he's young, from the way his voice sounds, and I know he must be young from the self-confidence he's got."

"How do you know that if you've never seen him?"

"Because he sounds so cocksure—no, that's not exactly the word. Positive? Authoritative, maybe. You know, the what-I'm-telling-you-is-the-absolute-truth bit. No ifs or buts to his sermons."

Gretchen pulled away then to laugh up at him and wrinkle her nose. "I don't like opinionated people."

"That's only an impression. He may not be like that at all. Shall we try it once?"

"Well—I suppose—What do the people look like who come out? Funny?"

"Hmm—two arms, one head, two legs—"

"David! You know what I mean. Sort of odd? Fanatical?"

"I must admit that was my first thought too. But a couple of families drive Cadillacs, there are some Lincolns, Olds—not that there can't be rich fanatics, of course," he added hastily. "But they look like normal people. The women look stylish—fancy hairdos and things. That's usually a pretty good sign of being normal, isn't it?"

She couldn't help laughing at that and then asked cautiously, "If I go once, you won't keep after me to go again?"

"Once will probably satisfy me too," he assured her.

When Gretchen wakened the next morning to a close, muggy day, she lay for a moment regretting her promise. It would be so much more fun to pack a picnic lunch and go for a drive and have a lazy day. She hated the thought of having to dress up and be with people she didn't know and listen to stuff she didn't believe. But David was already showering and she *had* promised, and there would be time to go for a drive in the afternoon. They could even eat dinner out since it would be too hot to cook. With a sigh she got up and went out to the kitchen to put on the coffee with no premonition of the nightmare the decision would precipitate.

TWO

THEN THEY WERE READY too early and sat in the living room looking at each other. Several times Gretchen started to say impulsively, "David, let's not go. It's too hot. We won't know anybody," but each time she stopped. He had gotten up to walk restlessly around the room, jingling the loose change in his pocket—a sign, she had learned, that showed his eagerness and anticipation. Though she couldn't share the eagerness, she didn't want to squelch it, especially since he had suggested out of thoughtfulness for her that they not go until the last minute so they wouldn't have to talk to anyone before the service and could sit in the back row and leave as soon as it was over.

They could hear singing as they pushed open the outer door and stepped into the large open area where chairs were arranged in rows facing a platform at one end of the room. David nodded toward two empty chairs near them in the next to the last row and guided her over with his hand under her elbow. There was a book on one of the chairs, and David leaned to pick it up. He nodded at the woman in the row ahead who half turned to show them the page number, and thumbed for it. As the others sang, Gretchen looked around curiously. There was no evidence of nursery school equipment except for two children's-size tables and several dozen small chairs off to one side of the room. Everything else must have been shoved out of sight behind the folding doors along the back of the room.

She looked at the congregation, amused at how accurate David had been in his description of the stylish women. Some of them could have been —well— She looked around. Not a Miss America certainly, but perhaps a Miss County Fair. She felt herself relax a little. Obviously none of them were cranks in funny clothes. Most of the adults seemed to be in their thirties and early forties, with a row or so of teenagers and a couple of dozen children.

She observed more than she listened, craning her neck to see what the minister looked like when he got up to preach. She couldn't resist nudging David. He was big with wide shoulders and large hands, one of which held a book—a Bible, she supposed—and the other gestured freely as he spoke. She could understand what David had meant by his voice, because it was filled with assurance—a listen-to-what-I-have-discovered assurance. But his manner made it clear that everybody could make the same discoveries about God because they were all in the Bible. She got that much before she stopped listening. David was absorbed in what the minister was saying, but there were too many interesting facets of the people around to distract her attention.

The two young children on the row ahead were quietly amusing themselves drawing stick figures of each other and covering their mouths to hold back silent laughter, with frequent sidelong glances at their parents who frowned warningly at them. The boy on the end of the second row who was chewing gum so hard his ears moved up and down in rhythm made her fight her own laughter. She looked at the row of teenagers on the other side about halfway back, most of them girls, and wondered how much they were really listening. She didn't know why she was so reassured by the fact that most of the girls wore short skirts, though she had to admit that some of them looked as though whoever had made the dresses had run out of material before they finished.

When the service ended, they had no chance to slip out unobserved but were overwhelmed by the friendly greetings of the people in the row ahead. One tall man, blond but with streaks of gray at his temples and sideburns, came over to talk to David. He had sat somewhere ahead of them, Gretchen remembered, beside a slender blond woman. Gretchen listened to his faint trace of accent as she stood slightly behind and to one side of David, decided it was Swedish, and moved closer to join the conversation.

As she did, the slender blonde came toward her, smiling. She held out her hand to Gretchen with a friendly, "Hello. It's nice to have visitors. Do you live near here?"

"Just around the corner and up a block or so."

"This is such a nice part of town with all the new homes and the young couples with children. We've noticed all the families in their yards when we drive by every Sunday." She laughed then. "This is so obviously the right place for a nursery school that we thought it would be a good place to begin a church."

"You don't live in this area then?"

"No, we're in the older section of town with conventional-type houses. I love to look at these new ones with all the bold, clever ideas the architects come up with these days." She stopped abruptly. "But here I am talking away, and you don't know us! I'm Gudrun Carlson, and this is my husband, Eric."

The men smiled. "Your husband and I have already introduced ourselves," David answered. "And we're Gretchen and David Marshall."

"You know, I just had a feeling your name would be David. No, really," she protested to their laughter. "I mean it. You look just like the kind of person whose name would be David. But Gretchen?" she pursed her lips and frowned. "You don't look like a Gretchen. You know—a Dutch blonde with round rosy cheeks and wearing wooden shoes." Her smile flashed as she spoke, and Gretchen was amused.

"If you're going by nationality, then, no, the name doesn't fit. I'm French and Irish, and I'm afraid I'm just as temperamental and emotional as that combination is supposed to be."

They had moved out the door as they talked and stood blinking in the bright sunlight where others of the congregation were still visiting. They were introduced to the minister, Paul Gorman, whose handshake left Gretchen wincing. When he moved away to speak to someone else, Mrs. Carlson turned to her husband impulsively.

"Bob and Janet can't come for dinner after all. I

wonder—" She turned back to Gretchen. "Could you—if you don't have other plans for the afternoon—won't you have dinner with us?"

"Oh, I don't think—" Gretchen began, her instinctive reluctance to be with strangers throwing up an automatic protective shield.

But to her surprise David cut in swiftly. "We'd like to. Though you know you're running a risk taking in perfect strangers."

"No, I can always tell when people are all right. Sort of a sixth sense," she answered. She looked around then. "We have a couple of daughters here somewhere. Yes, here's Sheila."

Gretchen looked at the slim, lithe blonde walking toward them, her hair glinting in the sun, and thought, *She's a genuine Scandinavian type*, and could imagine her doing a TV commercial for hair coloring. The girl stopped a few yards away and half turned to look back over her shoulder at the group she had just left. She waved and called back some laughing remark.

And then Mrs. Carlson said, "And here's Debra," and Gretchen turned to see another blonde exactly like the first, long shining hair, blue eyes, clear skin.

"Girls, this is Mrs. Marshall and her husband. They're coming home with us for dinner."

Gretchen smiled at the twins, liking the smiles they gave in return and their clean, shining appearance.

She wasn't surprised to find that one of the Cadillacs David had spoken of belonged to the Carlsons and anticipated that the "old conventional" house Mrs. Carlson had deprecated would be rather fancy.

30

And it was. It was the kind that Gretchen in her childhood dreams would have called a mansion. It was set well back from the street under trees that looked as though they had been there forever. A wide porch supported by thick white pillars ran the entire length of the house.

Mr. Carlson parked in the driveway and at the sound of the slamming car doors, a St. Bernard lifted its head lazily from the veranda, thumped its tail a few times, and then settled down again.

"A great watchdog he is," Sheila laughed and stooped to pat him affectionately.

Gretchen followed Mrs. Carlson through the door into the cool tiled hall and on into the living room, one part of her mind impressed by the wealth so evident in the furnishings, the other impressed by the gracious simplicity of their hosts' manners.

Her offer to help was dismissed with a quick "No, you're our guest. I left dinner cooking, and the girls have assignments. We'll be only a few minutes. Eric is going to catch the beginning of the ball game, and probably you'll want to also, Mr. Marshall."

In less than half an hour they were called to dinner, and Gretchen stopped in the dining room doorway to stare around her in frank appreciation. Wide French doors across the room led out to a sloping lawn completely circled by rose bushes. Inside the dining room on either side of the French doors a five-foot-deep garden curved back to each wall in two semicircles, each centered by a low fountain where water gurgled musically as it splashed out and down to mist the greens in the garden. At first Gretchen thought the garden actually extended outside, but then she realized that the walls behind the garden were covered with floor-to-ceiling mirrors reflecting the lime-green silk coverings on the other walls.

"How beautiful!" Beside her, David whistled softly, and Gretchen could hear his mind clicking out how long he would have to work to afford a room like this.

"Thank you," Mrs. Carlson answered. "My sister is an interior decorator, and we let her use her imagination here. We have never regretted it."

"I'll trade the conveniences of the architects you were talking about for the beauty of this anytime," Gretchen exclaimed.

She could feel her reluctance to come dissolving in the Carlson's low-key friendliness and in David's relaxed enjoyment of their company. Listening to the conversation and watching the personalities, she decided that no one could write a book around this family—at least not one that would sell well. They were too normal, the girls too polite and unsophisticated, their relationship with their parents too friendly to provide material for the usual psychological novel about family living that came across David's desk. She supposed the Carlsons would say it was because they all went to church, and decided she shouldn't be too prejudiced against the notion.

The twins, sitting opposite her, were reflected in the mirrored walls. Her first impression of their complete similarity began to fade as she saw the subtle shadings of each personality.

Sheila was the more vibrant of the two. In contrast

to Debra's mouth, which was a shade too narrow and pinched, Sheila's mouth was full and somewhat pouty, though it could flash quickly into an appealing smile like her mother's. Several times as Gretchen looked up from her plate she was sure Sheila's eyes shifted from her quickly, and she had the odd feeling that she was being measured. Then Sheila, apparently aware that her covert scrutiny had been noticed, smiled and said, "Since you've caught me looking, I'll ask. Is that a wig or your own hair?"

"Sheila!" her mother protested.

Gretchen laughed. "I don't mind answering. No, it's mine."

Sheila sighed. "It's neat! I don't want to cut my hair, but I'd like to wear it once in a while in that Dutch-boy style. It looks so—I don't know, sort of crisp. I've been after Mom to let me buy a wig in that cut, but she won't let me. She says I'm too young for a wig," she pouted with a half-smile in her mother's direction.

"No, it isn't that," her mother protested. "It's just that it doesn't seem necessary. Your hair is pretty as it is, so why cover it up with something false?" Mrs. Carlson lifted her shoulders slightly as she added with a little laugh, "I guess I'm just old fashioned. I can't convince myself to get one either."

Gretchen listened, amused at the thought of a sixteen-year-old these days asking permission of her parents to do something that simple. It confirmed her thinking that this family was definitely not novel material—unless as a throwback to archaic customs. But it was a refreshing change from what seemed to be

33

the modern accepted custom of the children bossing the parents.

She looked at the twins with a strange feeling of envy, and found herself thinking, *What would they have to rebel against anyway? They've got money, and looks, and love. They wouldn't have any reason to want a change.*

She came out of her private speculations to find that David had just finished telling how he had stumbled onto the church by accident.

"I suppose we really should have some kind of sign out front," Mr. Carlson said. "Though it's surprising how many people have mentioned that they hadn't even noticed the building was a nursery school even though they'd driven by it frequently. It's funny how the mind works—sometimes you see something but don't really see it."

David put his arm across the back of Gretchen's chair and laughed. "That's not my wife's problem. She has one of these camera minds. She sees something and click! She's got it forever."

Sheila leaned forward, her eyes shining as she looked at Gretchen intently. "You mean a photographic mind? Like you see a page of history dates and you can remember them? Jeepers, what a waste! You don't need a mind like that, and I do."

Gretchen laughed back at the envy in Sheila's voice and answered, "My husband is exaggerating. It's not really photographic. Sometimes I see something and it doesn't register at all at the time."

"What do you mean?"

Gretchen shrugged. "Oh, you know. You see some-

34

one doing something, and it doesn't mean anything at all at the time. Then later on its importance comes back to you."

"Like pieces in a puzzle," Mr. Carlson agreed. "My hobby," he explained. "I enjoy puzzles—the jigsaw kind. They relax me. But you can look at a piece and don't think it fits anywhere at all. Then you put a couple of other pieces in place and suddenly the first one fits."

As he went on talking, Sheila leaned toward her mother, and Gretchen heard her say in a low voice, "If we clear, can we go? I've got lots to do. And Jimmy's coming over for a little while—if that's all right."

Her mother hesitated and then answered, "All right. But don't go anywhere without letting me know first."

Gretchen was silently amused by the impatient gesture Sheila checked as she smiled around the table with an "Excuse me," and got up. She noticed too the glances the twins exchanged and was curious about the expression of—what?—spite?—triumph?—on Debra's face, as she picked up several dessert plates and followed Sheila.

Mrs. Carlson looked at Gretchen and smiled. "Don't let me discourage you, but raising children is not the easiest job in the world."

"I should think twins would be a lot of work."

"Oh, those first weeks," Mr. Carlson groaned. "Those night feedings were murder. It seemed as though we never slept day or night the first six weeks."

"When they are older though, twins are company

for each other. There's always someone to walk to school with you that first day and stick by you until you make your own circle of friends—which even twins need." Mrs. Carlson paused, a tiny frown showing a faint line between her eyes. "Sheila and Debra have always been very close. Oh, lately they don't seem to agree the way they used to. But that's part of growing up," she finished lightly.

Gretchen couldn't help wondering whether Jimmy was one of the things they didn't agree about and wondered too whether Debra had a Jimmy of her own.

"We have it easier than some parents," Mr. Carlson said, shaking his head. He began to tell of some of the problem juvenile cases he had handled, and Gretchen, listening, wasn't surprised to find that he was a lawyer. She could imagine the good impression he would make on a jury with his voice strong and yet mellow, his chin firm without being aggressive, and his wide smile which swept you into his confidence.

It was a pleasant afternoon except for the moment at the end when they were driven home. Mr. Carlson pulled the car to a stop in front of their house and asked, "Where do you usually go to church?"

Gretchen felt her muscles tighten. They weren't going to escape after all. She had been expecting to be preached at all afternoon, but they hadn't once mentioned religion. She had been lulled into a false sense of security by the Carlsons' apparently genuine friendliness and interest in them as persons, not as potential church statistics. Now she waited for David to answer and listened as he said frankly, "We aren't churchgoers. But we certainly found yours a friendly place to visit."

"Yes, and thank you for the dinner. It was nice of you to have us," Gretchen added, moving quickly from David's side toward the door. In her haste to get away, her purse slid to the floor, spilling open, and she scooped her belongings together and ducked her head to get out of the car.

"I hope they don't expect us to come every week," she said, watching the car drive off.

"We don't have to go just because they want us to. They *were* friendly though."

"Umm, yes. Rich too."

"You don't mind coming back to a cracker box with flowers growing outside instead of in?" He held the door open for her and she went in, shaking her head vigorously.

"As long as you come with it, I can do without the other fancy things." She kissed him lightly on her way to the kitchen. "Like something cold?"

He followed her out and got out ice. "He looked just the way I expected him to."

"Who?"

"The minister."

"Oh!" she laughed. "You mean he looks as bossy as he sounds? I thought he was rather mild-looking, though younger than I expected him to be at first when I saw how little hair he has. To be honest, I can't remember much of what he did say. I don't know that I listened that much."

"Because you didn't want to?"

She looked back at him thoughtfully. "Partly I

suppose. But also I wanted to see the people—what they were like. And, by the way—" She turned to look at him. "What was that business of saying I have such a photographic mind? It isn't true, but I couldn't very well call you a liar."

"You do remember things," he protested. "Every one of my faults, all the anniversaries I for—Hey! Cut that out!" and he ducked away from her threatening hand.

She hung sheets and pillowcases out early the next morning, already feeling the oppressive heat the day promised. Turning from the clothesline, she saw Brian across the two yards, sitting in his sandbox. His little blond head gleamed in the sun which reflected on his bare shoulders where the playsuit straps had slipped down. He always burned so easily with his fair skin that Ruth was a fanatic about leaving him out in the sun too long. That must be why she had put him out so early to avoid the bright sun later, and Gretchen smiled as she watched his serious absorption in filling a bucket with sand and dumping it over his legs.

When she went out later in the morning to bring in the already dry clothes, she stopped abruptly. At first glance she thought Brian was leaning over to scoop up sand. Then she could see that he had fallen asleep, his head resting on the hard edge of the sandbox. She stood irresolute, frowning as she watched him. Ruth was so edgy lately that she might not appreciate interference. Still, it wasn't like her to leave Brian out so long. And it wasn't good for him.

She called softly, "Brian," but he didn't stir.

From where she stood she could see the redness

creeping across his shoulders and down his bare back. Even if Ruth got mad, something should be done. She turned and went into the house and dialed Ruth's number, letting the phone ring ten times. When there was no answer, she dialed again and listened to the ring.

"Something is certainly wrong." The words rang loudly in the quiet of the house and made her turn abruptly and go out, cutting across the next-door yard. She patted Mixie as she passed him lying in the shade of his house with his tongue lolling out, and rang Ruth's back doorbell. She was glad the neighbors both worked so they wouldn't be curious. Brian had wakened and begun to cry as Gretchen rang the bell again and then tried the door knob, knowing it wouldn't open. Crazy Ruth was always locking the doors to be sure the wrong people wouldn't get in, even though Jack kept telling her that sometimes she might need help and no one could get to her.

Scooping Brian up, Gretchen carried him back across the yards and put him down in the middle of the kitchen floor with a cracker. Then she called the police station and asked for Jack.

When he answered she asked, "Is—was Ruth all right when you left this morning? . . . No, I don't know that there's anything wrong. But she's always so careful about Brian, and when I saw him out in the sun so long. . . . Yes, in his sandbox. . . . Oh, at least an hour and a half. . . . I tried calling, and I went over and rang the bell but she doesn't. . . . No, the door's locked. . . . I brought Brian over here. . . . Yes, I'll keep him."

She put the phone down and went out to Brian.

"Come along, sweetie, and we'll get some of the sand and heat washed off you."

Brian lifted his arms to her as she leaned down to pick him up. His lower lip trembled, and he said, "Mommy cry."

Gretchen frowned. He seemed to be saying this frequently lately. She wondered whether it was just a combination of words he had picked up, or whether he was telling what he saw. She washed his hot skin and gently rubbed Vaseline over the red places, gave him a drink of water and put him down in the middle of the double bed. He looked so defenseless lying there looking up at her that she felt choked with emotion. She was reminded oddly of the other little boy who had looked out at the world from the newspapers last week, but whose helplessness and innocence had not saved him from murder.

She sat beside Brian for a few minutes until he dropped off to sleep and then went out, closing the door softly. Glancing out the front window, she was surprised to see a patrol car parked in the street. Jack had gotten home sooner than she thought he would. She was sure he had gone first to check on Ruth and, since it was impossible to concentrate on doing anything, she waited nervously for what seemed an interminable length of time before she saw him striding up the walk to the front door.

She held the screen door open as he stepped inside. "I'm sure glad you noticed Brian."

"I am too. I was afraid Ruth had fallen and been hurt and couldn't get to the phone to call for help. She is always so careful of Brian. Is she—all right?"

He shook his head. "Not really. She isn't really —feeling well. She went back to lie down for a few minutes after putting Brian out and—fell asleep. She's—not sleeping well—" He turned his cap around in his hands as he talked, the lines around his mouth deep and grim.

Gretchen nodded. "I know. She has been worried. And the story about the little boy upset her—"

He threw out his hands in a futile gesture, interrupting her. "She's so emotional. She relates everything bad that goes on to us. 'What if Brian were kidnapped?' she says. 'What if you get killed?' she says. What if—what if? I tell her you gotta take the bad lumps with the good and go on living. But she doesn't see it that way. Everything bothers her. If I'm five minutes late getting home, she's uptight with worry. And then she—" He stopped abruptly, his hand on his hip, staring moodily out the door.

He turned then. "Look, would you be able to keep Brian for a couple of hours? I can get off early today. One of the guys owes me some time, and I can come home right after lunch. I think Ruth will stay asleep that long."

"Of course," she answered quickly. "I think he feels enough at home with me that he won't be upset. Several of his toys were left here the last time Ruth brought him over. We'll get along all right."

"Thanks," he said gratefully. "Where is he now?"

"Sleeping. Poor little fellow seemed worn out."

"I won't disturb him then. If he should be awake, he wouldn't want me to leave him, and you'd have trouble getting him settled again."

41

Gretchen followed as he opened the screen door and stepped outside into the hot sun and listened as he said suddenly and explosively, "You see so many rotten, cruel things in my line that it makes you—" He stopped, gripping his hat hard in his hands.

"That little boy?"

He nodded. "I was in the detail that found his body. Poor little kid." His face was hard with the bitter memory as he stared down the street through narrowed eyes. "If we ever find the rotten person who did it—"

Then he looked at her, his eyes asking for understanding as he said slowly, "If Ruth—oh, spouts off now and then—try to overlook it, will you? Things like this that happen—well, she can't help thinking—what if—what if it were—were—"

He couldn't finish and Gretchen nodded wordlessly, oblivious to the cars passing in the street, thinking only of the tragedies of life and the senseless cruelties of one human toward another.

Jack roused then and turned toward the patrol car. "I'd better get back. Oh, by the way, you won't need to—it won't be necessary to check on Ruth. I locked the doors and left her a note so she'll know where Brian is. She probably won't even wake up before I get back."

"The best thing for her is sleep. That fixes anything."

"Yeah. Almost anything."

Jack's tone was so bleak that Gretchen stared at him, at his brooding face and somber look. But before she could answer, he turned and strode to the car. She watched as he eased it down the street and turned the corner out of sight. She sighed, feeling pity. Poor Jack. What a tough job he had.

She stooped then to pick handfuls of purple and white petunias, Brian's favorite flower next to dandelions. They would look jaunty in the porcupine flower vase that fascinated him. She would have to do something to keep him from the pathetic "Mommy cry" that trembled constantly on his lips.

She had turned to go in when she heard a car stop in front of the house and looked back over her shoulder. One of the twins had gotten out of the car and was walking toward her.

"Mrs. Marshall, I'm—"

"Yes. Debra. How are you?" Gretchen smiled at her.

The girl looked at her in surprise and then blurted, "How did you know which one I was? People usually automatically say Sheila first. I guess because she's the one they think of first."

Her tone was unmistakably bitter, taking Gretchen by surprise, and she thought, *Maybe things aren't as smooth in their family as I thought from seeing them yesterday.*

But aloud she said, "People may look alike but everyone has his own personality, and that's the thing to go by." She looked toward the car. "Can you come in?" she asked lamely, hoping the answer would be no.

"We just came by to leave you this." She held out her hand with a lipstick in it and Gretchen laughed as she reached for it.

"So that's what happened to it. It rolled under the

car seat yesterday when I dropped my bag. But it really isn't important enough for you to bother bringing it over. I have others."

"That's all right. Sheila wondered where you lived. And she wanted an excuse to drive the car. We haven't had our licences very long," she added in explanation. As Gretchen looked at her, she was staring back toward the car and Sheila, her lips pressed so firmly together that it gave her a cross look, making her seem older than she was.

Gretchen wanted to say, "For goodness sake, loosen up! What do you have to be so sour about with all you've got?" But she didn't. She could remember her own dreary adolescence. Even for the twins in their security, it could be a time when there always seemed to be something that wasn't right—usually something little that seemed big. And if it wasn't really big, it was easy enough to make it loom large.

"Well, thanks again," she finally said as Debra stood awkwardly on the step, not seeming to know how to leave. She watched her walk to the car and waved at Sheila before going into the house.

It wasn't as easy to care for Brian as she had expected. When he wakened he was fretful, and she was afraid he had a slight fever. So she spent the rest of the morning rocking him and trying to coax him to eat a little soup and pudding. She handed him over with relief to Jack when he came about two o'clock.

"If Ruth isn't feeling better tomorrow, bring Brian over when you go to work," she suggested. "If she has the flu there's no use exposing Brian—"

"No, it isn't flu."

"Or I could come over there and take care of both of them—"

"She'll be all right tomorrow," he interrupted abruptly. "She's been under so much tension lately it's made her—sort of—go to pieces."

"Let me send something over for your supper tonight."

"No, thanks, Ruth won't be hungry, and neither will I."

Gretchen watched him walk down the street, carrying Brian with his little head burrowed against his father's shoulder and his arms circling his neck in a tight squeeze. She frowned, thinking of Ruth and knowing she ought to feel more sympathetic toward her. But all she could honestly feel was impatience at Ruth's inability to be mature enough to face life. Everyone had problems, and certainly many were worse than Ruth's, since hers came partly from her imagination.

Maybe she's expecting again, she thought suddenly and hoped not, knowing how Ruth would hate it. All too vivid were the times when she and David had been invited over for cards and had sat through an embarrassing scene. Somehow Ruth always got on the subject of how much she wanted Brian to have a brother or sister but how she wasn't going to bring any more children into the mess the world was in. And Jack always argued back until Ruth got up in tears and fled to the bedroom to check on Brian, leaving them waiting—Jack angry, Gretchen embarrassed, and David reading a magazine until the storm passed.

"How can they fight like that in front of company?" she had fumed more than once to David.

And he had shrugged, "I guess we're not company."

"But they do that no matter who's around," she had persisted. "And it's obvious they love each other. Ruth can hardly talk about Jack without getting maudlin over him. She's so worried about something happening to him, and it isn't only because of herself and Brian. He's the one her life revolves around. I tried to tell her once that Jack would be the one to live to be a hundred and have everyone asking him the secret of his long life, but she wouldn't laugh. She's sure he is going to be ambushed some day. From the things she's said to me, I gather she's nagging at him—and not too subtly—to leave the force."

Now with the picture before her of Brian secure in his father's arms, she remembered with a chill David's serious "She has a right to worry about his life. He's in danger every time he goes to work."

The thought bothered her the rest of the week. She didn't see Ruth except to wave at her once across the yards and call, "How are you feeling?"

"Fine," Ruth called back and disappeared inside the house.

Ruth did call early Friday and asked for a ride to the store. Since she made no reference to Monday's incident, Gretchen didn't mention it either. But Ruth's trembling hands as she lifted Brian into the car and her puffy eyelids and pinched expression made Gretchen regret her impatience.

"You should have told me you were getting all

dressed up." Ruth's voice was querulous as she looked at Gretchen's pale yellow cotton dress and sandals. "But I wouldn't have bothered anyway in this heat; and with all the humidity, shorts and a sleeveless blouse are the easiest things to put on and save a lot of washing." She stopped to push the damp hair off her forehead. "I hate summer when it's like this, and I keep telling Jack we've just got to get an air conditioner at least for the bedrooms so we won't have Brian fretting all night and keeping us both up. And Jack especially has to get sleep so he can work overtime so other people can sleep in peace, and then he keeps telling me of all the other people who have it so much worse than we do—"

The familiar bitterness ran on, and Gretchen wondered silently how Jack stood it if Ruth did this all the time when he was home. Maybe she didn't. *Maybe I'm her safety valve*, she thought wryly.

The salads and frozen dessert she had made early that morning and put in the refrigerator nagged at her accusingly. She *should* invite them over for dinner. There would be enough. But then—then she would have to listen to Ruth going on and on like this. And she wanted David to herself. *Maybe next week*, she promised silently, trying to listen again to Ruth's stream of words.

David was later than usual getting home, and they ate leisurely so that by the time they had finished dessert it was getting dusk.

"Let's leave the dishes and take a pitcher of iced tea out on the patio," Gretchen suggested.

A slight breeze stirred the treetops without really

cooling the air, but it was relaxing to sit companionably in the darkness, hearing the sounds of children going protestingly into the house to bed, and birds answering one another up and down the street as they settled for the night.

David lifted his head, listening. "Was that the doorbell?"

"I didn't hear—oh, yes, I guess it is." She wrinkled her nose. "I hope it's nobody you have to invite in. I'm too lazy to be polite to anyone tonight."

The doorbell rang again as David slammed the screen door behind him on his way through the house. In a moment he reappeared with a man she didn't recognize in the darkness until David introduced him as Mr. Gorman, and she groaned inside. Didn't ministers have any sense about making calls?

"Will you join us in some iced tea?" David asked, indicating the pitcher on the table.

"I don't need a second invitation," he replied promptly. "With lemon or without, sweetened or not, just so it's cold." He took the glass Gretchen offered, with a smile and a thank you.

The heat of the day and her conscience-pricking neglect of Ruth had left Gretchen feeling irritated. She had to force herself to be polite and smile in his direction when he looked her way to include her in the conversation. She wished he hadn't felt obligated to make his polite professional call. He could have saved his time and theirs too. And she wished David wouldn't bother being polite in return, finding similar interests in sports and fishing.

I'll bet he's good at finding out what people are

48

interested in and then pretending interest too, she thought cynically, though she had to admit that his big build and broad shoulders made him at least look athletic. *I wonder how long it will take him to beat around until he happens to remember why he came.*

To her surprise, he was direct. "I was glad to see you in church Sunday and want to invite you back again. Are you new in the neighborhood?"

"We've been here about five months."

"How did you happen to come to the church—since it doesn't fit the usual picture of what a church looks like," he finished with a chuckle.

David laughed too and explained, including his wanting to see what the minister looked like and see if he matched his voice.

"Did you get your questions answered?"

"Some. But you raised others."

"Maybe I can help you with answers to them too."

Gretchen listened to the conversation as it moved back and forth between the men, conscious of their easy acceptance of each other. She could sense that each one knew the meaning of what the other was saying under the surface words, and she felt left out.

Then Mr. Gorman asked, "Are you members of a church somewhere else?"

David shook his head but Gretchen spoke swiftly, surely, "No, we're not. We're not interested in religion. We never have been."

"Then you have never read the Bible?"

"No."

She knew her voice was challenging and rude, and she didn't care. This was an invasion of their privacy!

But he only smiled and said, "Too bad. If you aren't interested in religion, you're missing a fourth of your life."

To Gretchen's dismay, David leaned forward and asked, "How do you mean?"

"We all have four sides to us." He took a pen and notebook from his shirt pocket and drew a square. "One is physical, one is mental, another is social, and the fourth is spiritual. If you leave out the physical, you're dead. If you don't develop the mental, you're a dummy. Ignoring the social side only gets you ignored by other people. And if you ignore the spiritual side, you're not finished; you're incomplete even if you have the other three sides. Oh, you can get along on the other three, but there's a gap. And when you die and find out the spiritual *was* important, then where are you?"

He looked at them with a friendly smile as he asked the question, but the words hung in the air like a challenge. Then he stuck the notebook and pen back in his pocket. "You can say it's my job, of course, but I happen to believe that that fourth side is the most important. So when I see someone who is missing it, I want to share with them the best way I know to strengthen that side. I believe that a personal knowledge of God through His Son, Jesus Christ, is the only way this can be done."

And Gretchen thought, *All right, you've said your piece and done your duty, so now please go.*

But David cleared his throat as he leaned forward, studying his hands clasped loosely in front of him. "You—spoke of the Bible. I'm in the publishing business, so naturally I'm familiar with the Bible—from a business standpoint, that is. I know it sells, so people must read it. Books are my bread and butter—"

"It's interesting that you put it that way," Mr. Gorman interrupted with a smile. "That's just what Jeremiah said God's Word, the Bible, was to him —bread."

"And Jeremiah is?"

"A great writer. He said, 'Thy words were found, and I did eat them, and thy word was unto me the joy and rejoicing of mine heart.' He was a great prophet too. You ought to read his book. It's tremendous. As a matter of fact, I've got a copy in my car if you'd like to borrow it."

"Well, sure—"

"There are others too—great writers like Isaiah, Daniel—"

"Aren't they—" David frowned. "Oh. You mean the Bible then."

"If that bothers you, try reading them as men who were writing about the great issues of their day— as they were. You'll find them very contemporary. Very relevant." He stopped then and after a moment he shook his head. "You won't be able to read them as men. You'll see God in them because He is there. Just as He is in every issue of life today."

He stood up then. Gretchen smiled back briefly as he thanked her for the tea. She watched as he and David strolled around the side of the house, and she could hear David's voice asking a question and then the minister's voice in reply. She gathered up the glasses, wiping the wet rings left on the table and wadding the napkins, straightening the chairs automatically.

She had gotten along for twenty-three years and hadn't noticed any gap. And David hadn't either —until now. She frowned. There was no denying his interest. *Why did he ever have to find that church?* she thought crossly.

The men apparently had found much more to talk about, standing out by the car. Gretchen washed the dishes, wondering what they were talking about so long, and feeling uneasy. She had the kitchen straightened before David came back, a book in his hand, riffling its pages as he came through the house to the kitchen.

"It is a best seller," he said defensively in answer to her look. "I ought to be impartial enough to at least look at it."

She made herself smile back at his seriousness. "David Marshall, dealer in antiques," she teased and kissed him.

But he held her off and looked down at her. "You don't really like the idea, do you?"

"What idea?" she asked, sparring for time.

He gestured with the Bible. "My interest in this."

She considered her answer and then looked up, a smile crinkling her eyes. "If you find something in it written by a woman, let me know and I'll read it. OK?"

He laughed then and bent to kiss the back of her neck. "OK."

THREE

THE FIRST PHONE CALL came that night. Because it was so hot they had sat up watching the late movie. Gretchen had felt the need of something to relax her. In spite of her light words to David, she didn't like this new interest at all.

David was showering to get cool enough to sleep when the phone rang. Gretchen heard it at first with annoyance and then with the quick moment of alarm when a phone call comes unexpectedly at midnight. But when she answered there was no reply. She could tell the line was open, but no one answered her repeated "Hello?" She finally hung up in disgust but with a sense of relief. She had no relatives to hear bad news of, but David's parents could have sudden emergencies.

"Who was it?" David asked anxiously, coming out of the bathroom. "I had just turned off the shower when it rang."

"Wrong number, I guess," she yawned. "Or else some drunk who thought he'd called a cab or something and didn't know what to do when he realized he had the wrong number. Anyway, whoever it was didn't say anything at all when I answered. Just breathed."

"Usually a drunk makes the same mistake twice, so if it rings again, I'll get it."

The phone didn't ring again that night. But Monday afternoon just as she was starting dinner, it rang, and she answered to hear the same heavy breathing but no reply to her annoyed "Hello?" Then it happened again a half-hour later. When David came home she told him about it with a worried frown.

"Either someone is just doing this at random and happened to get us several times, or else someone has us mixed up with someone they think they're playing a joke on. Only, it isn't funny."

"If it happens again, we'd better report it," David replied. "But you can be thankful whoever it is doesn't say anything. It would be worse if it were an obscene call."

Before the end of the week, Gretchen wished whoever was calling *would* say something. The phone rang repeatedly at various times with only the same hard breathing at the other end. There were three calls Tuesday afternoon in quick succession, and she finally went out, in spite of the heat, to work in the yard where she wouldn't hear the phone. But she found it hard even to concentrate on weeding the flower beds and was glad when David came home, his suit coat folded over his arm.

He leaned over to drop a kiss on her cheek. "It's almost too hot even for that," he grinned.

"I know."

"Is it hotter in than out?"

"No, I just had to get out to get away from the phone."

"More calls?" he asked sharply.

She nodded and sat down in a lawn chair across from him. He got up to pull his chair more into the shade, tossing his coat over the back of another. It slipped to the ground and she caught at it, noticing its weight.

"What's in your pocket?" she asked, feeling for it. And then, "David! You haven't been reading this on the bus, have you?"

"Sure. Why not?"

"Don't—people—see you?"

"I suppose. I haven't been hiding it behind a paper." He was amused. "Is it indecent to be seen reading a Bible?"

"No, but—"

"Would you rather I read—oh, *Quotations from Chairman Mao*? Or—"

"Well, no! But still—"

"You think it would be more acceptable to be seen with books like that than with the Bible?"

"David! What is this? The third degree?"

"Well, is it?" he persisted.

"Not more acceptable—no."

"What then?"

"Well, more normal—or something. Certainly more intellectual."

He raised his eyebrows at her, and she flushed. "Well, maybe not the example you gave, but some books would be more intellectual. And yes, certainly more normal. I'll stick by that word."

He was silent, frowning across the yard. "Yes, I suppose you're right." Then he looked at her, leaning forward eagerly. "Honey, I don't understand how I've missed it all these years. There's this terrific story of Daniel—wait, listen to it." He picked up the Bible, looked in the index for the page number, and turned to it. "Here he is in danger of death if he prayed to God, and he does it anyway. It says he prayed to his God as his custom was, knowing he might die because of it."

"So he was brave," Gretchen shrugged.

He looked at her uncertainly and then down at the Bible. "I suppose so," he agreed slowly. "But I was thinking—he must have had a great God."

She heard the wistful sound of his voice but wouldn't let herself listen to it. All the rest of the week she worried over how they could suddenly be going such separate ways in their thinking. There was not only the tension of the insistent phone calls, but the sense that she and David were gradually moving into different worlds of thought on a matter which really was of such little importance.

She slammed the receiver down on the second call which came on Friday just after lunch and went to sit shivering on the couch in the living room, not even feeling the heat of the sun pouring in the front window. She couldn't define the sense of dread that persisted, even though she knew there had to be some reasonable explanation for the calls. She jumped then when the doorbell rang suddenly, not having heard anyone come up the walk, and went cautiously to the open door.

"Hello. I was in the neighborhood and thought I

would stop a minute." Mrs. Carlson looked at her brightly from the other side of the screen.

"Well, hello. Come in." Gretchen forced a smile but inside she groaned, thinking, *I suppose she's out checking. Why doesn't she mind her own business?*

She gestured to a chair, and Mrs. Carlson sat down on the edge of it, clutching her handbag. Gretchen watched as she smiled and then took a deep breath.

"Let me begin by explaining my visit. You see, the reason we began the church out here was to reach a new neighborhood. Now that we've been here several months, we're taking a survey of the families around us to see who might be interested in coming to church. I volunteered to do this block, since I know you."

Gretchen gave what she hoped was a polite smile and listened as Mrs. Carlson went on.

"So I'll just put a check by your name as being interested in church even though you can't always come. Now, what about your neighbors?" With pencil poised, she looked at Gretchen expectantly.

"I don't understand."

"Could you give me the names of any others on this block you think might want the minister or someone to call on them? People who aren't already going somewhere to church, of course."

Gretchen looked at her for a moment. Then in an even voice she said, "I remember how furious my aunt was once when someone gave her name to a salesman as one who was interested in a new vacuum cleaner. She did not appreciate being bombarded by persistent salesmen for weeks afterward. And I certainly will not do that to my neighbors."

It was not until she finished that she realized how icy her voice had been. She watched Mrs. Carlson's stricken face as she looked down at her notebook, turning the pencil uncertainly in her fingers. It was obvious that she had been completely unprepared for the blast.

She looked up then and stammered, "I'm—I'm sorry. I guess I didn't realize that you felt as—as strongly—I mean, well—church has been so much a part of my life. I don't—I can't imagine it not being so to everyone. It—it isn't then to you?"

"No."

"Or your husband?"

Gretchen looked away.

"Please believe me when I say I'm sorry," Mrs. Carlson pleaded. "I wouldn't dream of offending you—or your neighbors."

If she would just go! Gretchen thought silently. *Just go and not talk about it anymore.*

But it was apparent that Mrs. Carlson felt she had to give more explanations, and Gretchen listened unwillingly.

"You see, I'm—I'm really not good at this sort of thing. I don't meet people easily or find small talk coming naturally to me. My husband has that gift—I suppose he has to in his profession—but I don't. So it's very difficult for me to do something like this. That's why I thought since I knew you a little, I could do your block—" She stopped then and leaned forward earnestly. "This really isn't like selling vacuum

58

cleaners, Mrs. Marshall. If you saw a person dying of thirst and you had a glass of cold water, wouldn't you want to share it with him?"

"Yes, but if I saw someone with a glass of cold water, I wouldn't try to shove my glass of iced tea on him," Gretchen shot back. "I'd think he was perfectly satisfied with his water, and I would leave him alone."

In the silence the phone rang. She heard it and got up slowly. She picked up the receiver and listened a moment and then slammed it down and turned to face Mrs. Carlson.

"Is something wrong?"

"We've been getting phone calls. Only no one answers. It's made me edgy." She came back and sat down. If Mrs. Carlson chose to accept this as an explanation of her flare of anger a few moments ago, let her.

"Isn't there some way the phone company can trace them?"

"No. The man David talked to said the calls might even be coming from different pay phones. If it's the same person calling each time, he might even be calling from different sections of the city. Or else all the cranks in town are picking on us accidentally." She tried to laugh but failed.

"Can you have your number changed? Get an unlisted one?"

"David's checking on that today."

She felt then how dry her lips were. "Would you like a cold drink? Orange juice? Iced tea?"

Their eyes met then and suddenly they both laughed.

"Orange juice, please."

Gretchen went to the kitchen, relieved that the tension was lifted without the need of further explanations. She didn't want to take back anything she had said, but she was sorry she had spoken so sharply. Mrs. Carlson was too guileless to have meant to deliberately hurt or snoop.

She came back with the cold glasses and asked, "What do the twins do for excitement?"

"Swim" was the prompt answer. "They spend more time at the pool than anywhere else these hot days, though they don't actually do much swimming." She laughed. "Apparently the idea is to be there—where all one's friends are, I mean. Next summer they should get jobs, I suppose, if only to develop a sense of responsibility. But this summer—they're only just sixteen—we're letting them have fun." She added with a half-shake of her head, "It's hard to know if one makes a wise decision these days. You say yes to something—or no—and then you wonder if you said the right thing."

Gretchen was silent. Everyone should have an Aunt Phyl who said no automatically as far as Gretchen could remember, and never had any qualms or second thoughts about it. Probably the Carlson twins were spoiled. She looked at the dainty fragility of the woman opposite her and wondered if she had ever had to be firm about anything. Did she have any steel underneath her gentleness that would help her meet a crisis if one came?

But Mrs. Carlson was going on. "I am a little concerned about Debra. She's too much like me—too reserved. Sheila's so—oh—open, outgoing, so frank to talk about anything that bothers her, like her father." She smiled. "Maybe sometimes she's too frank, but that's better than keeping everything closed inside. Debra used to be more outgoing, but lately she has seemed—oh—closed in to herself. There are times when I feel she is just on the verge of confiding in me, and then she turns away."

"Does she date a lot?"

Mrs. Carlson shook her head ruefully. "I suppose really that's part of the problem." She looked across at Gretchen. "I mean the fact that Sheila has so many dates. She always has left what the old romantic novels called a trail of broken hearts ever since she was old enough to know the importance of a smile and the trick of batting her eyelashes."

She hesitated and a slight frown puckered between her eyes. "Lately Sheila has been dating one boy rather steadily, which bothers her father a lot. He really doesn't like Jimmy very well. Though I must admit that we haven't gotten to know him. He is always polite to us, even deferential."

Gretchen had a wicked impulse to ask if he went to church but knew that would be silly since he undoubtedly did. Apparently everyone they knew did.

Then Mrs. Carlson leaned toward her impulsively. "Maybe you've got answers. You're nearer the girls' age than I am."

Gretchen laughed as she shook her head. "Don't judge any other teenager by what I was. David was my one and only date. I never dated in high school, not once. I was never in the popular crowd. Hardly anyone even knew me."

"Did it bother you?"

She laughed shortly. "Of course. But I lived."

"I wish Debra knew that. It's so hard to know how to help her when she stays home all the time while Sheila is always out—or would be if we let her."

"Sorry I can't help," Gretchen answered, knowing she wouldn't want to even if she could.

"Well, thank you for the juice and for being frank. I never thought of a visitation attempt like this from your viewpoint." Mrs. Carlson hesitated and looked at Gretchen and then dug for her car keys. "Let me know how you come out on the phone calls," she urged. "If you do get an unlisted number that should take care of the problem."

Gretchen laughed. "David thinks it must be some author he's turned down who is trying to get even with him and is making us the object of a mystery story."

"The explanation is probably as simple as that, but I'm sure they must seem very frightening to you." Then, not quite meeting Gretchen's eyes, she said, "I hope my interference and bungling today won't keep you from coming back to church."

"Thank you. I shouldn't have lashed out at you. It's just that—well, you have your ideas and I have mine." But as she watched Mrs. Carlson drive away, she knew that David had his ideas too, and they seemed to be nearer the Carlsons' than hers.

He seemed to take for granted that they would go to

church on Sunday. Gretchen complied but was determined not to listen to the sermon. Instead she occupied herself by looking again at the rest of the congregation. She particularly looked for the twins and found them sitting with half a dozen other teenagers, Debra on one end of the row and Sheila in the middle, exchanging notes with the girls on either side.

When they were introduced to others after the service, one of the men shook hands with David and asked, "This may sound rude, but where do you people dig up some of the authors who write the books you turn out?"

David laughed. "I'll admit that some of them bring up a good bit of dirt with them." He shrugged. "Unfortunately, those are the ones doing the most writing. Or maybe I should say those are the books people want written, if you judge by the sales."

"People buy them, huh?"

"Bookstores are more than making a living. You know the idea—give the public what it wants. But I've got a lead on a couple of authors now that I'm going to visit this week. They seem to write a little cleaner than some."

"Too bad the clean ones are the dull ones."

David shrugged again. "Doesn't have to be that way," he said, and turned to talk to someone else.

Gretchen stood listening idly, noticing the age cleavage of the congregation. The high school crowd was lined up along the fence that ran along the side of the playground area. Debra's and Sheila's bright heads were clearly visible, and beside Sheila was a boy's figure, but she couldn't see him clearly. *That must be Jimmy*, she thought, and wondered where he had been sitting during the service. The children raced around between the talking groups until they were gradually corralled by their parents and herded into cars.

Gretchen smiled at the various ones to whom she was introduced, murmuring a polite hello but not attempting anything more. Her senses were alert as she saw the minister turn to David and heard him ask, "How's the reading going?"

"Isaiah is great, isn't he?" David replied with his quick, enthusiastic smile. "He sticks with you. Like the place he says—let's see if I remember it— 'Hast thou not known? Hast thou not heard, that the everlasting God, the LORD, the Creator of the ends of the earth, fainteth not, neither is weary? There is no searching of his understanding.'* I've never thought of the greatness of God before, of the power that He would have to have—if He is God."

"There's another side to God too. If you read on a chapter or so you find, 'When the poor and the needy seek water, and there is none, and their tongue faileth for thirst, I the LORD will hear them. . . . I will make the wilderness a pool of water, and the dry land springs of water.' "†

Watching the two men as they stood smiling at each other and sharing a thought pattern beyond her, Gretchen felt the rising tide of anger and loss. *He has no right to take David from me*, she thought jealously.

*Isaiah 40:28.

†Isaiah 41:17-18.

There must be *something* she could plan for Sundays that would be more interesting to David than church.

These thoughts were far from her mind as they drove to the airport the following day. Gretchen was already feeling lonely. "Do you realize this is the first time we've been separated since we were married?"

He nodded, reaching to grip her hand. "And I wouldn't go this time if there were anyone else to send. What are you going to do with all your free time while I'm gone these two days?"

"Make a dress. I won't have to stop and fix a meal and can just eat whenever I want to."

"Let Ruth know I'm gone, and she'll invite you over."

Gretchen made a face. "I know. But then I'd have to listen to a nonstop recital of her problems—real and imaginary—and that's too wearing."

"She has to tell them to someone."

"I know, but does it have to be me? I don't pour my worries out on her."

"You have some?" He looked at her for a moment and then back at the road.

She felt ashamed. "No, I guess not. Not like hers. All right, I'll be little Miss Fixit and go talk to her this afternoon."

After David had checked his bag, they walked toward the gate, Gretchen clinging to his hand, and stood at the window looking out across the runways. She saw the bulge in his suitcoat pocket.

"What are you reading now?"

"Poetry. It's beautiful stuff. Want to hear it?"

Without waiting for her answer, he turned toward

the row of empty seats by the window and pulled the Bible from his pocket. She sat down on the edge of the chair and watched as he thumbed toward the middle of the book and read,

He that dwelleth in the secret place of the most High
Shall abide under the shadow of the Almighty.
I will say of the LORD,
He is my refuge and my fortress:
My God; in him will I trust.

Surely he shall deliver thee from the snare of the fowler,
And from the noisome pestilence.
He shall cover thee with his feathers,
And under his wings shalt thou trust:
His truth shall be thy shield and buckler.

Thou shalt not be afraid for the terror by night;
Nor for the arrow that flieth by day;
Nor for the destruction that wasteth at noonday.‡

Gretchen sat listening as his voice read on, feeling cheated at having to share these last few minutes with the Bible when she wanted his attention for herself. But she managed to smile as he closed the book and put it away, held her close for a final kiss, and then waved back over his shoulder before disappearing inside the plane. She watched until the plane took off, though she couldn't see David, and then walked disconsolately back along the endless terminal to the parking lot and drove home. The house seemed abnormally quiet, which she knew was silly since David

‡Psalm 91:1-6.

66

was never there in the daytime anyway. But the whole city was lonely with him away. The kitchen clock which usually ticked off the minutes faster than she wanted them to, now seemed to be dragging. She got out all the patterns for sleeveless summer dresses and some of the material she had picked up from time to time on sales. But at the back of her mind ran the promise she had made David to talk to Ruth, and she decided she might as well get it over with. Better to listen to Ruth rant than to sit here trying to sew but thinking about David sitting on the airplane reading spooky poetry from the Bible.

Even though it was hot, she mixed a batch of brownies; and when they had cooled and were iced she went across the back yards. Mixie lifted his head to give an imitation growl as she passed, and she said, "Oh, go back to sleep, you lazy thing."

She rang the back doorbell and stood waiting, hoping she wasn't waking Brian from a nap. There was no answer to several more rings, and she stood irresolute. She knew that Jack had gone to work that morning, though he might have had time off and come home to take Ruth and Brian for the trip to the zoo he had been promising. Turning to go, she looked at the plate of brownies with distaste. She would have to come back later with them, or they would be stale before she ate them all. David didn't like chocolate, so there would be no point in freezing them.

She looked around uncertainly at the faint sound that came then. A child was crying. She listened at the door. It was Brian. *Ruth must be sick again*, she thought, and tried the knob, not really expecting the

67

door to be unlocked. The knob turned easily in her hand, however, and she opened the door to call, "Ruth?" The only answer was loud crying from somewhere inside the house.

She stepped into the kitchen, and one look was enough to let her know that something was wrong. To Ruth, yesterday's newspaper left in a chair today was clutter, and the sight of the kitchen now with breakfast dishes piled in a heap in the sink, a milk carton tipped over on the table with a pool of milk drying to a scum on the floor, made Gretchen put down the plate of brownies and hurry through the house. She followed the sound of Brian's crying to the bedroom and found him standing at the foot of his crib, his face streaked with tears, his nose running, and his breath coming in shuddering gasps. He held up his arms to her, and she picked him up, cuddling him to her and feeling the sodden wetness of his diaper against her arm.

She murmured comforting words to him, rocking him back and forth in her arms, and patting him until he began to quiet, though his breath still came in long sobbing gasps.

"We'll go find Mommy," she whispered against his warm neck and felt his chest heave with the deep breaths. Crossing to the other bedroom, she knocked on the door and then pushed it open to stare down at Ruth who lay sprawled on the bed, breathing noisily. The smell in the room was evidence enough that she had been drinking, even without the two half-empty bottles that lay on the floor just beyond her outstretched hand that dangled over the edge of the bed.

Gretchen stared down at her, instinctively shielding Brian from the sight of his mother in nightgown and robe lying in a drunken stupor across the unmade bed. Her first thought was to get her cleaned up and sober before Jack came home. Then she remembered his guarded behavior last week when she had kept Brian. Jack knew already. She had taken for granted that Ruth had been sick. *And she was*, she thought grimly. *This kind of sickness.*

The phone rang as she stood there, and she reached for it automatically. There was an instant of silence and then Jack said, "Gretchen?" Alarm colored his voice. "What's wrong? Is Ruth—"

Compassion sprang in her. She couldn't let Jack know that she knew Ruth's problem, so she said as casually as she could, "I just dropped in for a visit and happened to be nearest the phone. Do you want to hold on? Ruth can't come just this minute." She waited for his answer with a feeling of panic and turned away in revulsion from the sight of Ruth's openmouthed breathing and tangled hair. What would she do if he said yes?

But she was sure there was relief in his voice when he answered, "No, I just wanted to let her know I'll be late for supper." He gave a quick, hard laugh. "In fact, I'll just let you tell her. That way she can't blow her top at me. Tell her—tell her to go ahead and eat, and I'll pick up something before I come home. That way she won't have to try to keep something hot, because I don't know exactly when I'll be there. She won't like it, but—"

Gretchen could picture his worried, defensive face,

and she said quickly, "Don't worry. David is away, so I'll invite myself to stay. I'll stay until you get home," she reassured him.

But the assurance drained away as she put the receiver down and went to stand beside the bed with Brian, who was patting his mother's cheek. Gretchen felt anger and disgust at Ruth's weakness.

"The first thing to do is get you dried off," she said to Brian, who looked up at her with his lower lip and chin puckering.

"Mommy cry."

"Yes, I know. She doesn't feel well. Come along with Auntie Gretchen and we'll put some dry clothes on you."

As she pinned dry diapers on Brian and put him into a clean playsuit, she tried to think what to do to sober Ruth quickly. Black coffee was what they always did in books. That and dousing them with cold water. She'd try the coffee first, and maybe Ruth would come to enough to take a shower and get herself cleaned up.

The next hour and a half were a nightmare as she made strong black coffee and tried to shake Ruth awake enough to drink some of it. Brian stood solemnly watching, and Gretchen wondered if his limited vocabulary would be sufficient to tell his father later what had happened. Or worse still, if this would be the picture of his mother he would carry through life.

Probably this isn't the first time she's been like this and won't be the last, she decided grimly and wondered why she had never suspected that Ruth was an alcoholic. Maybe because Jack harped so against drinking anything stronger than beer—and maybe this was why.

But when Ruth finally came to enough to gulp down two cups of coffee and be aware of her condition, she dropped her head in her hands and cried huge, shuddering sobs that wracked her whole body. Gretchen's disgust gave way to pity and she sat down beside Ruth on the edge of the bed and put a comforting arm across her shoulders.

"How can I stop? When I got married I promised myself and I promised Jack that I would never take another drink and I hadn't, even though it's been hard, so hard, but lately things have gotten so awful, and I'm so worried about Jack and I can't sleep, and I imagine every day that Brian is going to have to grow up without a father. And so I got started again one day, thinking I was just going to have one tiny drink, just a little sip one evening after Brian was in bed and Jack was late getting home. He hadn't been able to phone me, and I could see him stretched out on a sidewalk or crumpled beside his squad car with a bullet in him or dumped in an alley, and I couldn't stand it—" She broke off to wipe futilely at the tears running down her cheeks.

Gretchen bit her own lip and looked down at Brian as he stood anxiously beside his mother, his own lower lip puckering to cry. She leaned over to pick him up but he wiggled away, his eyes on his mother, and held up his arms to her.

"Ruth! You've got to pull yourself together. You're frightening Brian. Go take a shower, and I'll fix us

71

some supper. We can talk later when Brian isn't around to hear."

"He's too little to understand." Ruth sat on the edge of the bed, her shoulders sagging and her hands plucking nervously at the edge of her thin cotton gown.

"If he says 'Mommy cry' enough times to Jack, he'll ask why. Do you want him to find out about this?"

Ruth jerked erect and squinted through red-rimmed eyes at the clock.

"No! I promised him last week I'd never do it again. And he'll be home soon. Gretchen, help me!" She stood up, clutching at Gretchen and swaying dizzily.

"Jack called. He won't be home for supper—"

Ruth's eyes were enormous in her thin face as she licked her dry lips and asked fearfully, "Does he know—did you tell him—"

Gretchen shook her head. "I just said you couldn't answer right then, and he asked me to tell you he would be late. I told him I'd stay and eat with you. I don't think you should try to shower, or you might fall. Take a bath and wash your hair."

Gretchen guided Ruth's stumbling feet into the bathroom and ran bath water for her. Then she went back to the bedroom and stripped off the sheets and pillowcases, putting them in the washer. She vacuumed the rugs and sprayed cologne around the room.

When Ruth came out of the bathroom, she was white and shaken but looked more like her fastidiously clean self. Gretchen was alarmed at the way her bones showed as Ruth zipped herself into shorts and a sleeveless blouse.

"Have you had anything to eat today?"

Ruth frowned, thinking. "Not since breakfast I guess. I did fix Brian lunch," she said defensively, flushing under Gretchen's gaze. "I had only had one little drink then, but I sat down to keep him company while he ate, even though I wasn't hungry, and then I got thirsty and thought I would just have one little drink more and then—" She stopped and threw her hands out in a helpless gesture. Then she turned away and asked in a low voice, "Where was Brian—when—when you came? I—I don't remember—"

"In his crib," Gretchen replied quickly. "You had taken care of him. He was safe. But frightened," she added then sternly.

The tears came again with Ruth's gratitude. "Thanks, Gretchen, for being so kind and not blaming me when you could, you know; anyone could who didn't understand all the worries I have—"

"Dinner's ready," Gretchen interrupted to shut off the sound of the thin, whining voice running on and on.

Ruth followed meekly and ate ravenously without talking, giving Brian what he needed, but concentrating most on satisfying her own hunger. When she finished, she shoved her plate back and leaned her elbows on the table, resting her chin on her hands. Even though her fingers were laced together, Gretchen could see how they trembled, and she wondered how much of it was nervousness and how much from the effects of her drinking.

"Thanks, Gretchen," she said again simply. "I can't tell you how much I appreciate your sticking with me and not letting on to Jack that something was wrong when I must have looked horrible, just horrible."

"The worst thing was seeing Brian stand there wondering what was wrong. Jack could understand what made you do it, but the baby couldn't."

Ruth's eyes filled with tears again. "I know, and I promise myself and I promise Jack and I even promise God—if there is one—that I'll stop; but then, it's the only way out that I've got, it's my only escape from all my worries, the only way I can forget my problems. I do it because of my worry about Jack and Brian, don't you see?" she pleaded.

Gretchen was silent. She wanted to tell Ruth that she drank because it was easier than facing up to her problems and trying to live with the worries. But she was sure it wouldn't do any good. Ruth had enough guilt feelings as it was without piling on any more.

She got up and began to help clear the table. Ruth's trembling fingers spilled the sugar and, in brushing it up, knocked a cup on the floor, shattering it. The tears came easily again, slipping down her cheeks silently.

Gretchen, touched and yet embarrassed by so much emotion, said gently, "Why don't you take Brian out in the yard since it's cooler, and I'll do the dishes? Please do," she added, brushing off Ruth's protests. "Brian needs you. I'll come as soon as I've cleaned up here."

Ruth went without more arguing, and Gretchen watched from where she stood at the kitchen sink as Ruth put Brian in the sandbox and then sat down on the edge, helping him make roads for his little cars. From this distance, in her shorts and blouse, she looked more like a sixteen-year-old than the drunken, disheveled woman she had been that afternoon. Gretchen worried as she washed and dried the accumulation of dishes. Ruth needed help, but where could she get it?

The uncomfortable thought crossed her mind that if she believed the little she had heard the minister say, God was the ultimate source of help for any problem, the only one with any power to help. But she didn't believe it, and neither did Ruth. So that was out.

When she joined Ruth, sinking into a lawn chair with a sigh of appreciation for the cool evening air, they sat together without talking. Gretchen didn't want to talk anymore about the afternoon and was thankful that Ruth seemed too drained by the day's experience to be able to worry out loud. Brian was on his mother's lap, leaning against her drowsily, her chin on the top of his head.

It was dark when Jack came, the car headlights flashing across the yard and lighting it as he pulled into the driveway and ran the car into the garage. He walked toward them with long strides.

"Everybody waiting for me?" he asked, his eyes going first to Ruth and then moving to include Gretchen in his smile. With a booming, "Come here, young man," he picked Brian up with a swoop and held him, squealing with delight, above his head.

"Did you have an emergency?" Ruth asked, and Gretchen noticed that the relaxed note had gone from her voice and the strain was back.

75

He shook his head. "Nope."

"What was it then? How come you had to work late?"

"Just routine," he shrugged.

"Is there anything new on that little boy?" Gretchen asked, regretting the question the moment it was out when she saw his hesitation. This must be what he was trying not to talk about.

She stood up quickly but Ruth asked, "Is there? Have they found who—"

"Oh, they think they have a new lead," he answered reluctantly. "But it isn't definite, and they're keeping it under wraps."

He turned to Gretchen then. "How long will David be gone?"

"Just until Wednesday morning. He comes in on a morning flight." She turned to Ruth. "Thanks for the invitation for supper."

"What? Oh—oh, yes—you're welcome."

"Let us know if you need anything," Jack called after her as she crossed the driveway to take the shortcut across the back yards. She stopped as she heard Mixie's low growl, and laughed back at them over her shoulder.

"I'd better go around to the sidewalk and up to the front door. If I cut across the yard, old Mixie will get all excited."

"Yeah. I don't think he's got any teeth but he sure can make a lot of noise when it isn't necessary. Let a real burglar come though, and he'd lick his hand."

"Jack!" Ruth protested. "You'll make Gretchen nervous."

"If I need you, I'll yell," she laughed back and waved good night.

She walked down the driveway and turned along the sidewalk, passed the in-between house, and then cut across the grass toward the front door. As she approached the house she stopped suddenly and looked back over her shoulder with the uncomfortable feeling that someone was watching her. She hadn't really heard anything, and no one was in sight. And even though it was dark, she was sure she would be able to see or sense a figure on the sidewalk. She could feel the pulse beating in her throat and shook her head. This was silly! Doors were open all up and down the street, with snatches of TV programs and music floating out and mingling in comfortable neighborly sounds. Birds were giving last-minute chirps in the trees overhead. It was a night like any of the others they had lived on this street.

Yet the uneasy feeling persisted and was heightened when she suddenly remembered that she had left the doors unlocked when she went over to Ruth's because she had only planned to stay a few minutes and it had been daylight then. She hurried up to the front screen door and pulled it open and stopped. She had left the inside door standing open. She stood hesitating on the step. If she went over and asked, Jack would be glad to come back and put on lights. But that was silly. How many times as a girl had she come home alone to the huge apartment building without being frightened? And now she was a grown woman and this was a safe, respectable neighborhood of families with children and no maniacs running around loose. Besides, it would only alarm Ruth if she called Jack.

She went into the house quickly, closing and locking the door behind her and then quickly unlocking it, feeling unreasonable panic. If there were someone in the house, she didn't want to be locked in with him or it. Keeping one hand on the doorknob, she groped for the wall switch and flipped it, lighting the lamps all around the living room, thankful for the ingenious device she had so far considered a toy but not thought of as a lifesaver. She listened intently without moving from the door.

There was no sound in the house, and the feeling of eyes looking at her had left. She hurried quickly through the house, turning on lights in every room, locking windows, and pulling curtains and draperies to shut out the dark and any prying eyes. Then she locked both doors and turned on the television. It was still too early to go to bed, and David had said he would call if his meeting didn't run too late.

She was thankful for the loud laughter accompanying the programs and kept the television on until time for the late movie, intending to watch that too since she could sleep late in the morning. But when it started, she found it was a horror show, and she got up abruptly and turned it off. Her imagination was too vivid already without giving it something to feed on.

It was obvious now that David wasn't going to call, and in a way she was glad, not being sure she would be able to keep him from knowing that she was frightened. When she had showered and was ready for bed, she stood for a moment by the window. It was really too hot to keep the drapes closed, and yet she was afraid to open them. After a moment she turned out the light, yanked the drapes open, and slipped hurriedly into bed, pulling the sheet up for a feeling of security. She had hoped she would be tired enough to fall asleep immediately, but instead found herself lying wide-eyed and tense.

The neighbors must all be in bed, for no light was reflected through the windows, and there were no sounds on the street. Gradually her muscles unlocked and her mind relaxed. The quiet was soothing.

Then in the silence came the sound of movement in the shrubbery outside the window. It was so slight at first that her mind drowsily whispered, *It's the wind*. But it was repeated, and her moment of drowsiness vanished as she felt her muscles tense again. It wasn't the wind. Someone was out there. There was definite rustling and movement just outside her window. *If only the bedroom were on the other side of the house*, she thought in fright. Mixie was not much help, but he might at least bark and scare off whoever was there.

She lay rigid, listening. The noise stopped then, and she licked her dry lips and felt the clamminess of her hands. She turned her head to see the clock. Almost two—a long time until it would be light. She tried to tell herself that it was only imagination. After all, she had never lain awake by herself in the house to know what the night sounds were. It was surely just the wind blowing the branches of the shrubs against the house. Tomorrow she would go out and trim them back, or the paint would come scraped off at that spot.

But as she reassured herself, something brushed

lightly along the window screen, moving back and forth from one side to the other. It made a whispering sound which could not possibly be from the shrubbery. Her mind whirled as she fought panic. If she called the police, whoever it was could slip away when they heard the police car, and she would be put down as a silly, neurotic woman. If she called Jack, Ruth would be more fearful of Brian's safety than ever. Whatever was done, she would have to do herself. But what could she do? she wondered as she listened to the soft scraping. If she went to investigate, she would come face to face with whatever it was.

Finally she crept stealthily out of bed and over to the window. Reaching suddenly, she pulled the window down and locked it, yanked the drapes together, closed and locked the bedroom door, and leaped back into bed. She lay in a cold sweat, listening to the words scrabbling over and over in her mind, "Thou shalt not be afraid for the terror by night. Thou shalt not be afraid for the terror by night—"§

"But I am, I am," she whispered.

She lay trembling, listening to the clock ticking off the minutes and feeling a curious sense of desolation. It would be this way if she didn't have David—if he were gone forever. She squeezed her eyes shut and covered her mouth with trembling hands. Finally toward dawn she sank into an exhausted sleep.

She awakened about nine, feeling drugged from the oppressive heat of the airless room. She dragged herself wearily out of bed and showered. Then, putting on the coolest outfit she could find, she went out

§Psalm 91:5.

and looked along the side of the house. At first she almost scolded herself for her overactive imagination, for there were no footprints to show that anyone had stood outside her window in the dark. But as she knelt, pretending to weed around the bushes in case curious eyes were watching, she stopped suddenly, cold chills making bumps on her arms. There *had* been someone there! The footprints had been smoothed over, but she could see traces of them. And there were places where small branches of the shrubs had been broken off by the weight of someone standing among them.

She stayed there on her hands and knees staring at them. She had not worried about David being gone because with the new unlisted number there would be no more phone calls. Now she wondered if there was a connection between the calls and the night visitor. But there couldn't be. The phone calls were simply the work of a sick mind, and this—this was probably just a Peeping Tom, serious as that was.

After all, she didn't really know any of their neighbors except Jack and Ruth. Any one of them could have some kind of quirk. And any one of them could have seen David get into the car with a suitcase and then have seen her come home alone.

She hurried inside, suddenly unreasonably suspicious of the soldier who she knew was home on furlough across the street and the retired man, out for his usual morning stroll, with whom she had previously exchanged greetings.

Her tired body ached to lie down, but she knew she didn't dare take a nap, or she wouldn't sleep that night. And she couldn't risk another night of sleeplessness. If she were tired enough and were safely locked in, she might sleep and not know if there were noises in the bushes or against the window.

To pass the time and try to get her mind off the dread of spending another night alone, she went shopping after lunch, intending to get so tired from walking through the stores that she could not possibly stay awake. Engrossed in trying to decide which pair of shoes she wanted, she looked around as a familiar voice said, "Do you do this kind of thing too? Wait until you have to buy for a couple of teenagers!"

"Hello." Gretchen smiled back at Mrs. Carlson and then widened the smile to include Sheila.

"Actually, Sheila is helping me buy this time. She thinks I need educating on what the current shoe style is. Aren't some of them ghastly?" She held up several and laughed, and Gretchen nodded, tried to suppress a yawn, and didn't succeed.

She looked her apologies and said, "I'm sorry, I didn't sleep very well last night. David's away, and this is the first time I've been alone, and I kept hearing things in the night."

"What kind of things?" Sheila asked curiously.

"Oh, they were probably imaginary." She shrugged. "The wind sounded like someone in the bushes looking in the window." As she said the words she knew she was only trying to convince herself that she hadn't seen remnants of footprints. "If it hadn't been for those phone calls, I probably wouldn't have paid any attention to it," she added to Mrs. Carlson.

"Phone calls? What phone calls?" Sheila looked at her curiously. Then she caught her breath. "You mean those kind where people say terrible things?"

Gretchen shook her head. "No, fortunately not that. But they were bad enough." She felt kind of silly explaining them to Sheila, whose eyes were wide with curiosity.

Listening, Sheila shuddered. "I'd have been scared to death. Couldn't you just not answer?"

"I tried that several times but the phone just kept ringing. The only way to stop it was to answer."

"Do you still get them?"

Gretchen shook her head. "No, we have an unlisted number."

"Look," Mrs. Carlson said impulsively. "Would it help if one of the twins came over and stayed with you tonight?"

"Oh, I don't want to bother—"

"You would, wouldn't you, Sheila?" There was just the slightest trace of pressure in her voice, and Gretchen caught Sheila's evident beginning of a protest.

She interrupted, "Please, no! Don't bother. Really, I'll be all right."

But it was too late, for Sheila said reluctantly, "Well, sure, I guess." Then more eagerly, "Sure, I'll come. Can Jimmy take me over?"

The question was a plea to her mother, who hesitated, frowning, and then said slowly, "Well, yes. I don't think your father will object to that. If he just takes you over and doesn't stay, it won't count as a date."

"What time shall I come?"

"Just whenever you want to after dinner. But really, I am imposing on you—"

Sheila shook her head. "I think it will be fun." She grinned impishly at Gretchen. "Maybe you've got some new makeup ideas I can learn. Or maybe you'll let me watch the late movie. My folks never do," she added with a pout.

At Mrs. Carlson's suggestion, Gretchen reluctantly gave her unlisted phone number. *I just hope she doesn't pester me to death,* she thought, irritated.

Gretchen had to admit she was relieved not to be alone for the night, though she didn't know what help a sixteen-year-old would be. And the thought of having to listen to teenage jargon all evening was nauseating. She could only hope the girl was a television addict. And at least they wouldn't have to share the same room.

Her frown deepened. This friendship could prove to be very annoying if Mrs. Carlson insisted on running her life. "I wonder if she does that with her daughters," she mused. "She'll have trouble if she does."

FOUR

GRETCHEN ANSWERED the bell when it rang about nine that evening and stared in dismay at both Sheila and Debra, each with a small overnight case.

"Hi," Sheila said breathlessly, her smile flashing but her eyes pleading for understanding. "I hope you don't mind that both of us came."

"Well—no." Gretchen held the screen door open. "Come in."

She hoped she was successfully hiding her annoyance. She hadn't wanted Sheila in the first place, and now to have to put up with them both was too much. Debra's expression was so sour as she followed her sister in that Gretchen wondered why she had come. She certainly didn't look as though she wanted to be there.

"Let me show you the bedroom," she began.

But Sheila interrupted with a quick, pleading, "Mrs. Marshall, do you mind if I run out real quick for just a couple of minutes and say good-bye to Jimmy? He brought us over and wanted to wait until we got safely in. He—he was kind of worried about the neighborhood when I told him what had happened to you last night."

"Oh, really, he needn't be," Gretchen answered, half in exasperation. She went to the open door and looked out, wishing she could wave at him reassuringly. She could hear the throb of the motor, but the car was only a shadow in the darkness, and she turned back to the girls.

"Tell him this is a perfectly safe neighborhood. And one of my close neighbors is a policeman whom I could ask for help if it were really necessary."

She caught Debra's expression and thought, *My goodness, the girl looks scared to death. I'll probably have to sit up with them half the night to keep them from being frightened.* She wished again she had not mentioned last night's incident.

"I promise I'll be right back," Sheila repeated and slipped out the door.

"Do you want to take your things into the bedroom?"

Debra had moved over to the open door and was staring out but jerked around as Gretchen spoke.

"No, I'll—I'll wait for Sheila. She won't be long. Dad said Jimmy isn't supposed to stay."

And Gretchen thought again, *Poor Debra. She needs a boyfriend of her own so she won't be jealous of Sheila. And poor Sheila, too, if she gets spied on like this all the time.* Debra was so obviously peering out the door toward the car, trying to see what Sheila was doing.

The phone rang, and she answered it to hear Mrs. Carlson's apologetic "I *am* sorry, Mrs. Marshall! When Debra heard that Sheila was going to stay with you, she simply insisted on going along. I told her you might not have room for her, but she said she could sleep on the couch or on the floor. Shall I come for her?"

"Heavens no!" Gretchen didn't care if the impatience she felt showed in her voice. What was the matter with the woman anyway? Why didn't she show a little spunk and simply tell Debra to stay home in the first place?

She listened to the helpless laugh Mrs. Carlson gave as she went on, "I guess you've sensed that Debra is jealous of Sheila. She didn't used to be. It's something that's developed just recently, and that's why it's so hard to know how to cope with it. I guess it's their age, and we'll just have to live with it until they outgrow it."

Debra would have to be blind and deaf not to know that the conversation was about her, Gretchen thought. She was embarrassed for them all and said briefly, "Don't worry. Everything's fine."

As she went back into the living room, Debra moved suddenly away from the door to sit down on the edge of a chair. In a moment Sheila's quick steps could be heard on the walk; and she came in, her face flushed and her eyes shining.

"Thanks so much, Mrs. Marshall, for letting me talk to Jimmy. He said he would stay in his car all night and keep watch, but I told him I didn't think you'd like that."

"That was nice of him," Gretchen answered, thinking herself ungrateful to be annoyed at the earnest offer of help. "I'm sure there's nothing for him to worry about."

She glanced at Debra, to find her staring at Sheila, her lips compressed in the tight line that seemed to be her usual expression. *It's too bad*, Gretchen thought, watching her, *that her parents let her go on turning what really is a pretty face into a jealous mask.* Then Debra picked up her case and went into the bedroom which Gretchen had pointed out. Sheila followed and closed the door. From the living room Gretchen could hear the murmur of their voices. She couldn't distinguish which was which, for they sounded so much alike. But they were apparently having an argument, for one of them said suddenly and passionately, "But you promised! You said you wouldn't."

Poor Sheila, Gretchen thought again with amusement. *Apparently she knew Debra was watching her.*

But when the girls came out of the room a few minutes later, the argument must have been settled, because Sheila's face was relaxed and her smile as warm as before, and Debra looked less sour and tight-lipped.

Gretchen wondered where to begin a conversation, since she had so little in common with them. It wasn't that she was so far removed from them in age, she thought as she watched them cross the room toward her. But her life as a teenager had been so different from theirs. And they would have no similar interests now since she had no background of church to draw from.

She looked up at them from her magazine and said, "Look at television if you would like, or find something to eat. I'll probably go to bed before you do because I'm still exhausted from last night." As a polite afterthought she added, "Or I'll talk if you want to." She smiled across at them.

Sheila answered the smile. "Oh, Mrs. Marshall, I—we—didn't come over to be entertained. We came over to be of help to you. We want to—well, protect you."

Her smile was bright, and the words were innocent of double meaning, and yet Gretchen felt anger and resentment rise in her at what they implied. She felt herself flush from the effort it took to keep from showing her anger and forced herself to sound relaxed.

"Perhaps we should get a little bit acquainted then. Tell me about yourselves. You're juniors in high school?"

They both nodded.

"Any special major? For what you want to be when you're through school?"

"Deb wants to be a nurse. Me? I haven't decided."

"It has to be something that doesn't require any work." Debra's voice was angry, and Sheila laughed.

"You see how well Deb knows me! I may be able to fool other people, even my parents, but not my twin."

"You can't expect to fool people forever."

Gretchen looked from one to the other. Debra's voice was low and even and controlled now, but Gretchen sensed there was a meaning behind the surface words that she didn't understand. There seemed to be an undercurrent between the girls, one accusing and the other attempting to defend herself. Debra was sitting at one end of the sofa, her feet on the floor, her arms folded, with her hands clenched tightly into fists. Sheila on the other end of the sofa had her legs tucked under her, and with her soft blond hair falling over her shoulders, she looked about twelve years old.

Sheila nodded back at Debra and gave a helpless laugh. "I know." Then she looked at Gretchen. "You see, Mrs. Marshall, we're alike in lots of ways, but we're different too. Debra is the one with the brains. Plus lots of perseverance. I give up too easily, so poor Deb has to try to pound the facts into me. The thing is—well, she's so smart she scares off the boys, and because I'm such a dumb little bunny, well—" She stopped and gestured in an appealingly helpless way.

She looked innocently unconscious of the sting in her words; but Gretchen looked back at her shrewdly, wondering how often she rubbed it into Debra about her lack of dates while seeming to play up her own weaknesses.

Deciding it was time to change the subject, she asked, "What do you do for fun?"

Sheila hesitated before smiling across at Gretchen. "I suppose what we think is fun is different from what you did at our age. Not that you are really *that* much older," she added quickly with an embarrassed laugh. "But you probably had fads that we don't and we have some you didn't, so—"

"Of course, we're different from a lot of kids our age because we go to church," Debra broke in abruptly, not looking up from the magazine she was leafing through.

"Sure," Sheila agreed quickly. "A lot of our activities are geared around the church. Not just this one, 'cause there aren't many kids our age who go

90

there. I mean the one we went to before. We still go to a lot of stuff there."

Gretchen looked at them curiously. Were they really all that much for church? Or did they go because their parents made them? She studied them through narrowed eyes and then asked abruptly, "How important is your church or your religion, or whatever you want to call it, to you?"

She looked at Sheila as she asked the question, expecting one of her quick, breathless answers. But Sheila was frowning, biting her lip and absorbed in thought as she stared at the paper she was creasing and uncreasing. Then Sheila looked at Debra.

"How can we explain it?" she appealed. "How can we tell her how important it is to us?"

"I only can tell her for myself," Debra retorted.

"Well, OK. You go ahead first then."

Gretchen sat looking at them as Debra began to talk, aware once again of the undercurrent of animosity between the girls and wondering which one of them was the stronger character. She'd been inclined to think it was Sheila, since she so obviously had the most personality and was the most outgoing. But now, seeing them together, she wasn't so sure her first judgment had been right. Debra seemed to have the ability to withhold comments and then to strike in a devastating way at a vulnerable spot. Sheila's barbs were covered with sugar while Debra's were laced with sarcasm, yet both got the desired result. Whatever they believed hadn't made them friends—at least not now—even though they were sisters. And she began to wonder whether there might not be novel material here after all.

At the moment Sheila was subdued as she sat listening to her sister and watching her meekly. Gretchen found it difficult to take her attention off the appealing picture she made as she sat curled up on the couch, her bright eyes fixed on her sister in rapt attention.

"And of course if you really believe this—I mean, that Jesus Christ is the only way to be saved—and if you accept Him as your Saviour, then you have to show your belief by the way you live. I mean, you can't just run around and do anything you want to because you or someone else thinks it's cool. There has to be a difference between you and other people. Not—not just in what you *say* you believe, because anybody can say they believe. It has to show."

Though Gretchen had missed most of what Debra had been saying, she could tell how intense had been her answer because her cheeks were flushed and she leaned forward in her earnestness. It was interesting to see, too, how basically shy she was, because instead of looking at Gretchen directly, she had said everything to Sheila.

Then Sheila shifted and laughed in a moment of embarrassment and turned to Gretchen with an apologetic, "I'm sorry. If we keep talking this way, you'll never want to go to church again. Especially ours."

"Oh, no." Gretchen shrugged indifferently. "Everyone is entitled to his own viewpoint on this subject as well as any other. We don't have to dislike someone just because we don't agree completely on everything. Your parents are very friendly people." She smiled. "Your father and my husband have hit it off well together. They've already had lunch together one day."

Sheila laughed indulgently and nodded. "Dad sees everyone as a potential mission field. He always says there are more heathen right around us than there ever were in China." She stopped, put her hand over her mouth for a moment, and then added hastily, "Not you, I don't mean. I mean—oh, yow! Now I've done it. Honestly, I didn't mean that you and your husband—I mean, you're not heathen just because you don't go to church very often. I mean—" She stopped completely then and looked helplessly at the floor, her cheeks flushed with embarrassment.

Gretchen's instant flare of resentment gave way to amusement at Sheila's confusion. *This was one trouble with the young*, she thought, watching Sheila's flushed face. *They confuse tactlessness with honesty*. But at least Sheila had the sense to recognize when she had been insulting, even if she recognized it a little too late. And it had not been deliberate.

But the thought of coupling David with the heathen was a little too much, and she particularly resented it since she was sure this was just what Mr. Carlson did think. Fortunately the phone rang in the silence that stretched between them; and she rose to get it, noting with amusement Sheila's involuntary movement to answer it.

It was David, and she was thankful for the long cord which let her escape into the bedroom to avoid being overheard. She didn't want him to know that the twins were there, or he would wonder why; and she was determined not to worry him with her fright of last night. His call only made her more lonesome and sharpened her annoyance at the twins' presence. She decided that, rude or not, she would tell them she was going to bed.

When she went back to the living room, she could tell they had been having another argument and found a malicious satisfaction in knowing that, for all their interest in church and religion, it didn't seem to help them get along with each other. But then, she mentally shrugged, she'd had enough psychology to know about sibling rivalry and that it was all a part of growing up. Even church didn't eliminate that, she was sure.

They looked at her expectantly as she said, "If you girls will excuse me, I'm going to bed. Get something to eat or drink if you want, or watch television. Sleep as late as you want to tomorrow."

Sheila looked up at her timidly. "Mrs. Marshall, I'm—sort of expecting a call." She darted an apologetic look at Debra and added a quick, "Jimmy just wanted to check on us. So if the phone rings, shall I get it? I don't think it will be late."

"Of course. And if there's a call for me, just take the message—unless it should be long distance, of course."

"Do you get up early? I mean, do you want us for breakfast at any certain time?" Debra asked. "Not that you have to fix us anything, because we don't usually bother with breakfast in the summer."

"You can do as you like in the morning. Just look for what you want in the refrigerator and cupboards if I'm not here. I'm going to run out and do some shopping about nine o'clock because I have to pick up my husband at the airport later in the morning. I'll just go out the back door to the garage and won't disturb you. If I'm not back and you decide to leave, go out the back door and close it after you, and the lock will set. Good night." She hesitated then and added what she hoped was a gracious-sounding "And thank you for coming over."

She smiled at them as they politely scrambled to their feet. As they smiled back there was a watching quality about them, particularly about Sheila, whose expression revealed her thoughts more clearly than Debra's. Gretchen found this disconcerting. She felt a generation apart instead of less than ten years and thought, *No wonder people go on so about not being able to communicate with the young. They don't give you much encouragement.*

She went into her room and closed the door firmly enough that they could hear it and could relax, knowing she wouldn't be overhearing their talk. When she went into the bathroom a few minutes later, she could hear the television and smiled to herself at how low they had it turned.

I'll bet they don't keep it that low at home, she thought and again was amused but irritated at their too obvious deference to her. *I suppose I should consider it politeness, because they have obviously been well trained as far as their manners go. That's something to be thankful for.* She remembered the couple she had seen in the car. Somehow, though, some of Sheila's politeness seemed put on. *But then,* she thought contritely, *maybe this isn't being fair. Maybe it was youthful embarrassment on Sheila's part.*

When she was stretched out between the cool sheets, the windows wide open to catch the cool breeze that had suddenly sprung up after the heat of the early evening, she was aware of how exhausted she was. The thought crossed her drowsy mind that the windows were open, but somehow it didn't seem important. She felt safe tonight and slipped off at once into a deep sleep. She wakened at some point during the night to the sound of water running and decided the girls were getting ready for bed. She didn't even bother raising her head to see the time, but turned over, gratefully glad that it wasn't time to get up.

Later she wakened again and saw a thin line of light under her door. A light was on somewhere in the house. She sat up and groped for the clock. Four-thirty. The girls must have forgotten to turn out a lamp. She automatically got up to investigate, pulling a thin robe around her as she opened the door. The light was faint and coming from the kitchen. As she went toward it, she realized that it was not the overhead light but only the small stove lamp. She snapped on a light in the hall in passing and thought she heard the tiny click of a door closing. But as she reached for the light switch in the kitchen, she saw Sheila leaning against the refrigerator door, looking startled and guilty.

"Oh, Mrs. Marshall! I'm—so—sorry!" she stammered, and the panic evident in her voice made Gretchen realize how much of an ogre she must seem to the girl. "I couldn't sleep, and I thought if I had something to drink maybe it would help. I didn't mean to wake you." Her voice trailed off miserably, and she stood clutching the carton of milk against herself and looking pleadingly at Gretchen.

"Help yourself," she answered. "The glasses are in the cupboard behind you. Fix yourself some cocoa or get a soft drink if you prefer." She moved toward the refrigerator, and Sheila took a step backward.

"Oh, no, thanks. This—this is fine. I'll just pour myself a small glass."

She reached to pull open the cupboard door, and Gretchen could see her trembling hands. She couldn't keep back an impatient, "Sheila, for goodness sake! Don't look at me as though I were going to snap your head off. I told you to feel at home."

Sheila flushed and blinked her eyes rapidly; and Gretchen thought with an exasperated sigh, *If she cries*—

But Sheila turned to stare out the window over the sink. Finally she seemed to get a grip on herself and reached for a glass and poured it half full of milk. She sat down at the table and smiled shyly up at Gretchen.

"You don't have any trouble telling us apart, do you? Most people wouldn't have been sure which one I was, but you knew right away that I was Sheila and not Debra. Are you good like that at other things?"

She was talking rapidly, concentrating all her attention on Gretchen, who answered, "Like what?"

"Oh, you know. Observing things, remembering.

One of my teachers is always saying, 'Don't just look—see!' I never notice things about people—their actions or mannerisms and stuff. Deb is much better at that than I am."

Gretchen poured herself some milk, got out a box of crackers, and sat down across from Sheila.

"Tell me something about your generation. Are you all really as different as all the newspaper and magazine articles make out? Are you all rock fans and fad followers and drug users? Or is that true only of kids who don't go to church? What are all you young people really like?"

Sheila listened to the questions with a little frown on her face and then bent to pick up her napkin as it slipped to the floor. In straightening up, her arm hit the glass of milk which slid across the table. Sheila grabbed for it frantically but only succeeded in knocking it off the edge where it fell, sending drops of milk skittering across the polished floor.

Sheila dabbed at the drops with her napkin, her big blue eyes filling with tears. Traces of the mascara she hadn't completely removed before she went to bed left smudges down her cheeks. "Honestly, Mrs. Marshall, I'm sorry! I'm just making a mess of everything," she wailed.

"It doesn't matter—" Gretchen began.

"What's going on?" The voice from the doorway was slow, blurred with sleep.

"What made you wake up?"

Gretchen looked up, startled at the note of fright that was still in Sheila's voice as she looked at Debra, and thought, *I never saw such emotional kids. I never got upset over every little thing that happened when I was their age. Maybe because I knew it wouldn't do any good.* And she could imagine what Aunt Phyl's reaction would have been if she had showed tears as readily as these girls did.

Debra's voice was still fuzzy-sounding as she asked again, "What's the matter? What's wrong?"

"Nothing is wrong. The floor is so well waxed that the milk will wipe up easily; and the glass didn't break, so there's no danger of anyone getting cut. Sheila, stop worrying about it," she finished sharply.

But Sheila only shook her head and ran out of the kitchen back to the bedroom. Gretchen looked at Debra and smiled ruefully. "I'm sorry if I sound impatient, but really Sheila is making something out of nothing. She isn't the first person to have spilled a little milk."

"Milk?" Debra repeated, struggling through sleep to understand. She rubbed her eyes. "What was Sheila doing with milk? Why was she up?"

Gretchen shrugged. "She said she couldn't get to sleep and came out to get something to drink to help relax her. I happened to wake up and came out, and we were talking. But the milk didn't help any because it spilled before she had a chance to drink any," and she gestured at the floor.

Debra's eyes focused on her then, and she frowned, obviously still not understanding all that was going on. Then she turned abruptly and threw back over her shoulder a quick "I'd better see how she is."

It wasn't until she heard the bedroom door close

behind Debra that Gretchen realized neither one had offered to help wipe up the milk.

"I wonder if they have to do *anything* at home," she muttered as she got wet towels and cleaned the floor and scrubbed off the wall where some of the drops had splashed. When she had rinsed the glasses, she turned off the lights and stood for a moment in the darkened room, frowning to herself. Some faint memory at the fringe of her mind seemed important, but it wouldn't come to the surface enough to be a definite thought. She yawned and went back to bed, hoping Sheila was settled for what was left of the night.

The sun was streaming in her bedroom window when she awakened again, and she stretched and sat up, smiling to herself. "All's well with the world," she said to the walls whimsically. "Just a few hours until David is home."

She dressed quickly, not bothering to shower for fear of wakening the girls. Anything to keep from having them under foot so soon. She made a grocery list while having coffee and toast and planned a dinner menu. It was going to be a blistering day according to the weather report she had turned on low. It would be too hot really to make a lemon meringue pie, but nothing was too much to do for David today. If she got to the store as soon as it opened and was home by ten, there would be time to make the pie before leaving for the airport—if she could keep the girls out of her hair. Maybe they would leave early.

She tiptoed through the hall to the bedroom for a

quick application of makeup and lipstick and got her wallet. Stopping in the kitchen for the grocery list and a carton of empty soft drink bottles, she softly unlocked the back door.

The promise of the heat that was to blanket them for the rest of the day was evident as she stepped out and gently pulled the door shut. She stopped for a moment on the porch to snip off the morning glory blossoms that were drooping in the heat. Then she shifted the carton of bottles to her left hand, tucking her wallet and the key case between the two rows of bottles to leave her right hand free to pull up the garage door.

She started along the driveway, glancing over at Ruth's yard. Brian wasn't in his sandbox yet, and she stopped, worried. That could mean that Jack wasn't on duty and they were sleeping late. Or it could mean that Ruth was sick again and Brian was standing at the end of his crib crying. She hesitated. Should she go over? And what excuse could she give Ruth if nothing were wrong? It probably would be better to wait until she came home, she decided, and started toward the garage again when the sudden scream came.

"Mrs. Marshall! Watch out! Stop!"

The scream checked her steps so suddenly that she lost her balance, lunged forward, felt the thin wire that grazed her legs just above her ankles as she fell against it, and then felt the cement of the driveway as it scraped her knees, tearing her hose. The bottles slid out as she dropped the carton, some of them shattering as they hit the hard cement.

Gretchen sat in the driveway dazed, rubbing

stupidly at her hands which she had thrown out instinctively to break her fall. She looked around as first Sheila and then Debra came tearing out the back door in their pajamas and robes, their hair in huge rollers.

Sheila reached her first and squatted down beside her, her eyes enormous in her white face as she cried, "Oh, Mrs. Marshall, are you all right? Oh, how awful! Look at your knees and your stockings!" She looked at something lying on the driveway among the broken glass and pointed. "Look," she whispered. "Look at that!"

Gretchen stared at the wire. Where had it come from? It wasn't there yesterday. And how could it trip her just lying on the driveway? But she had felt it across her legs—

Sheila had straightened up and walked partway across the yard.

"Look," she gulped. "It's fastened over there. See? Around the trunk of that little tree—down near the ground."

She pointed and Gretchen followed with her eyes but couldn't see it until Sheila leaned over and picked the wire up and jiggled it up and down.

"And look over here. A stick was pushed into the ground on this side of the driveway. The wire is fastened over here too." It was Debra who spoke, staring down at the ground and then over at Gretchen. Her voice trembled, and she suddenly hugged herself, shivering.

The gesture made Gretchen aware that she too was cold, though she was sitting on warm cement in bright sunlight. Her legs were trembling now in relief that the accident had been no worse. But suddenly she caught her breath. Accident? No! First there had been the phone calls, then the attempt to get into the house, and now—this.

Sheila apparently had been quick to see the connection too, as she stood staring at the end of the wire. She dropped it quickly and rubbed her hand on her pajama-covered leg.

"I hate to say this, Mrs. Marshall, but it looks like—well it could be someone is trying to—I don't know—scare you—or something."

"But—who?" She looked around and then back up at Sheila again. "Who would do something like this?" She shuddered. "If you hadn't seen it—I could have broken my leg, been badly hurt—"

"How did you happen to see it, Sheila?" Debra was winding up the wire as she asked. Gretchen watched, fascinated by the thin, now harmless-looking thing that someone at some time during the night had deliberately fastened across the driveway to make her fall.

"I can't believe it yet." Sheila's voice was thin with fright as she went over to sit down on the porch steps. "I heard you in the kitchen, and then you came back down the hall." She frowned, trying to remember. "Then you went to the kitchen again and I heard the back door open. I remembered you'd said you were going to shop and I was afraid you'd think you should hurry back just for us. So I got up to tell you not to hurry. You had already closed the door, so I looked out the window. Since I could see the garage door, I knew I would see you when you got there. But you didn't come right away—from the side of the house, I mean. I guess you stopped or something."

Gretchen nodded, remembering, "I stopped to pull off a few dead flowers." She gestured at the morning glory vines beside Sheila.

Sheila went on slowly. "So I waited, kneeling on a chair by the window, and while I was looking out I saw a bird—a robin—sitting in the backyard. Only I couldn't see that he was sitting on anything, you know? I mean, it looked as though he were just sitting in the air. I mean, birds can fly in air and all that but they can't just stand still in the air, can they? And I couldn't figure it out. Then I saw him sort of swaying back and forth and I couldn't figure that out either— what he could be sitting on, I mean."

She stopped to look at Gretchen and gave a tiny smile which disappeared immediately in the scared shiver that shook her.

"I've always had too much imagination. I—I can't even hear a ghost story on Halloween without getting scared. But all of a sudden—kind of in a split second—I thought about those phone calls you got, and I thought about your thinking someone was trying to get into the house, and I thought maybe this was a string or something to trip you. I couldn't see if there was another end someplace, because I couldn't see all the way across the driveway. Really I couldn't see anything at all. But I decided to yell anyway," she finished simply.

"It's lucky for me you did!"

"I would have felt awful silly if there hadn't been

104

anything there," Sheila admitted ruefully. "Not that I'm glad there was," she finished hastily.

Debra leaned over to help her, and Gretchen got up stiffly and hobbled over to sit down on the step beside Sheila, leaning her head against the side of the house. Her knees throbbed now, and she knew she should go in and wash them off and put on some medicine, but she still felt weak with relief and fright.

"Oh, you're all bloody!" Sheila covered her face with her hands.

Gretchen stretched out her legs, grimacing with pain, but said, "Oh, no, not much. My stockings are ruined but they protected the skin a little. I'll go in after a minute and put on some ointment."

Her resentment at the girls' coming had completely drained away, and she felt only gratitude which she tried to express. But Sheila kept her face turned away, and Gretchen had only a glimpse of her strained, white expression.

"She can't stand the sight of blood. It makes her sick," Debra explained in answer to Gretchen's questioning look.

Gretchen got up slowly, holding Debra's arm as she helped her into the house, leaving Sheila sitting forlornly on the back step. Gretchen's mind was numbed by the realization that someone had deliberately tried to hurt her. But who? And why? Then a more frightening thought came to turn her flesh cold. What would he—they—try next? How could she possibly protect herself against an unknown enemy who was striking at her for unknown reasons?

The girls had gone into the bedroom to dress, and

she could hear the subdued murmur of their voices. She looked at the clock. There wouldn't be time to shop now. By the time she changed and took the twins home, it would be time to meet David. On the way to the airport she would decide how to tell him all that had happened. They would have to decide whether they should go to the police.

The thought of the police reminded her that she had planned to check on Ruth. But it would be better not to call her now. Ruth's sensitive ears would detect the nervousness she was sure she wouldn't be able to keep from her voice. She would wait until she was back with David.

The twins were sitting in the living room with their overnight cases when she came out, and she managed a smile at them.

"I'm not a very good hostess not even to offer you breakfast."

They both shook their heads in protest, and Sheila said with a shiver, "I couldn't eat anything if I wanted to. I can still see that wire, and you falling and almost getting killed."

"Oh, Sheila!" Debra's words were angry and contemptuous. "Don't be so dramatic!"

Sheila's lips trembled. "I can't help it if I'm such a chicken."

Debra ignored her and looked at Gretchen. "You don't have to bother taking us home. We can call for a ride."

Gretchen found it an effort to smile back at Debra, appalled at her lack of sympathy for Sheila. But she answered, "It's right on my way. I'll drop you off at home and go on to the airport. Wait in front while I get the car."

"I could call Jimmy, but his car is in being fixed."

Debra whirled to look at Sheila. "Since when?" she demanded.

"Since early this morning. He had an appointment."

What else Debra said was lost as they went out the front door and Gretchen locked it behind them. She was impatient again at their inability to keep from arguing about the most trivial matters. What difference did it make to Debra when Jimmy took his car in? Gretchen was beginning to feel that the unseen Jimmy needed protection.

The girls were quiet on the drive home, and Gretchen was thankful. Her panic was subsiding with David coming home. He would know what to do.

"Thanks, girls," she said as they got out of the car. "Let me know if I can do something for you sometime."

She drove off, glancing back at them in the rearview mirror. She shook her head as she turned the corner and they were lost from sight. Maybe some twins thought alike, but not those two.

FIVE

As SHE DROVE to the airport, she decided not to say anything to David about the past two days' experiences until after dinner. It wouldn't be fair to pour everything out until he had had a chance to relax and talk about his trip. But she knew she would have to tell him before dark, before the shadows threw long, strange shapes across the yard and before the bushes began to rustle and whisper along the side of the house. She knew that if it were not for the wire this morning, she would still be trying to convince herself that it had been the wind in the bushes the night before. She shivered at the memory and gripped the steering wheel tighter. It was not so much the fact that the wire was there that made her turn cold, she knew. It was why it was there. And the anxiety of who had put it there.

Then another thought made her look around in sudden panic. How foolish she was to be driving this way alone, as though nothing were wrong. Anyone could be following her. And what better place for a seeming accident than the highway! Her eyes anxiously sought the rearview mirror and the other cars on the road. How could she tell if one were being driven by an unknown enemy? She drove carefully, keeping an anxious watch all the way to the airport. She parked as near the terminal as possible.

Reaching for the door handle to get out, she checked the movement and watched tensely as a car pulled in after her and parked two spaces over. The man behind the wheel was looking at her, and she pretended to search for something in her bag. He got out after a few minutes and she watched him walk away, feeling the pulse pounding in her throat. She waited, wondering if he were standing out of sight behind another car, waiting for her. She watched as another car cruised along slowly and finally found a parking place near her. She saw with relief that it was filled with children who piled out, hopping in their eagerness to see the planes. Quickly locking her car, she followed close behind them, hurrying along the endless concourse to the gate where David's flight was scheduled to come in. She chose a chair which she was sure was within full view of the flight reservations clerk and sat down on the edge, looking nervously around at the people waiting nearby.

Once someone stopped beside her just beyond her line of vision, and she started up from the chair and whirled around. It was only a man hurrying by who had stopped momentarily to light a cigarette and who looked at her curiously as she stared wildly at him, clutching her purse tight against her like a shield.

It was this nervousness that made her rush at David when he came through the gate and throw herself at him with a choked cry, forgetting her resolve to be calm.

"Oh David! I'm glad you're back!"

"Well, I am too—if only to get this kind of welcome. Maybe I'd better go away more often."

"Oh, no! No! Don't ever go again! Not without me!"

He held her off then and looked down at her. "What is it, Gretchen? Something's wrong."

She nodded and clung to him, her face buried against his coat. "I can't tell you now, not here. Let's go home. I'll tell you on the way."

And so as he drove, his hands tightening on the wheel and his face growing still as he listened, she poured out her fright.

"I wouldn't think anything about it if it weren't for the wire. I mean, I *could* have imagined everything else. Even the repeated phone calls could somehow have been accidental. But the wire wasn't. Someone had to fasten it there. It was there on purpose. And that means that somebody is purposely—purposely trying—" Her voice was shaking, and she stopped.

David was frowning. "But *why*? And why *you*?"

"Someone has me mixed up with someone else. That's the only explanation there can possibly be. Is there someone else in town with a name like ours— that must be it," she exclaimed eagerly, feeling a great wash of relief. "As soon as we get home let's look in the phone book. Not that we'll know what to do, but at least then we'll know it isn't us they're after. Why didn't we think of this before?"

"Who's the *they* you're talking about?"

"I don't know. But *someone* has to be doing this. I don't believe in ghosts."

But David said soberly, "Even if this is a case of

110

mistaken identity, if Sheila hadn't seen that wire—"
He broke off to reach over and grip her hand, and
Gretchen nodded bleakly.

But there was no other name even remotely like
Gretchen or David Marshall listed in the phone book.
There wasn't even any other name with a similar
enough combination of letters to be considered a pos-
sibility. She put the phone book down, feeling
cheated. She'd been so sure this was the answer.

David was standing by the front window, frowning
out, and she went over to stand beside him.

"Who are our neighbors?"

Gretchen looked up and down the street at the
modern houses with well-kept lawns, and flowers
neatly bordering the driveways. Almost every house
had children's toys in the garages, baby buggies or
strollers parked by the doors. Family people lived on
this street—decent people, kind people. None was a
maniac or a psychopath.

But how do you know? a part of her mind whispered. *You don't know what secrets may be locked
away behind the cheerful flowers and the sheer curtains.* Then the picture of Ruth lying across the bed in
a drunken stupor flashed before her, and she thought
dazedly, *I don't really know her either.*

She listened as David asked, "Is there anybody
you've spoken to—at the store or while you were
walking along the street or hanging out the
clothes—who seemed different? Is there anything
that might give you a clue? No one has said anything
strange or acted peculiar?"

She shook her head. "No, nothing. I've hardly

111

talked to some of the people on the block."

"Maybe that's it. Maybe someone on the block thinks you've slighted him—or her."

"But I've always answered anyone who spoke to me. That nice old retired man on the corner who walks by every day. He's so shy and gentle. He couldn't possibly do something like this." She hesitated. Then, "This is awful, but there *is* that soldier on furlough—"

She watched as David shook his head. "No, he left a couple of days ago. His father takes the same bus I do and was telling me about him."

She was silent, thinking. "Well, why does it have to be someone on our block? Why can't it be—oh, someone you've talked to—or haven't talked to?"

She stopped abruptly and looked up at him. "In fact, why are we so sure *I'm* the one someone is out to get? Maybe it's you."

"It has to be you. You're the one all this has been directed at."

"But they'd be getting at you if they got me."

"Hmm. You're right. I hadn't thought of that."

"After all, you're the one the wire might have been intended for, since ordinarily you go out to the garage first in the morning."

"Except I wasn't there."

"But who knew that?" she countered swiftly.

He shrugged. "Everyone at the office. Jack and Ruth—"

"And the Carlsons and the twins. The man you told

112

at church—and other people who heard you say you would be away."

"Plus everyone in the neighborhood who saw me get into the car with a suitcase." He tried to grin. "The list of suspects grows."

But somehow in the bright sunlight and with David home, the problem didn't seem quite as frightening and hopeless, and Gretchen groped for reassurance as she said, "Maybe it's all just coincidence after all. Maybe there's some perfectly logical explanation that we just aren't seeing. I'm going to try to forget about it."

He looked worried as he shook his head. "What explanation can there be for the wire?"

"There isn't any, I suppose." She looked back at him. "I know we can't ignore it. But where can we start looking for an explanation? We have no clues, nothing to go on. I haven't any idea who hates me."

Her tone was so forlorn that David pulled her close and sheltered her, his eyes troubled.

Finally he said reluctantly, "Well—let's wait a day or so and see if something else happens." He looked at her and his concern showed in his face. "Be careful though. Keep the doors locked, and don't let anyone in unless you know who it is. Wait until Saturday to shop, and I'll go with you. Don't take any unnecessary chances." He held her tight, and his voice was rough and choked. "I can't have anything happen to you."

"I'll be careful," she promised, tears close to the surface. She stayed in the house the rest of the day, going out only briefly to sit in a lawn chair in the middle of the front yard. But there were no trees there

113

for shade, and it was too hot to stay out long. Her only contact with anyone was a phone call to Ruth on Thursday morning. After listening to the usual flood of worries and complaints, she hung up to walk restlessly around the house, feeling sure she would forever have sympathy for caged animals. She looked at the pattern she had pinned on the material Monday—how long ago it seemed! Then she flipped through the cookbook looking for new dessert ideas, leafed through the vacation folders David had brought home, and suddenly got up again to walk aimlessly through the house. If she could only settle down to doing something, it would help, but she was too edgy to concentrate for long on anything.

She knew it was this feeling of restlessness that made her accept Mrs. Carlson's invitation later that day, an invitation she ordinarily would never have considered.

"It's a luncheon meeting tomorrow at church," Mrs. Carlson explained. "Not at our new little place but at the old church. I think you'll enjoy the program. It's to be music."

Gretchen agreed to go, thinking with a flash of amusement how glad David would be that she was voluntarily going to church.

Then she said, "Thanks again for letting the girls come over the other evening."

"They were glad to do it. Being together like that helped them too, I think. Anyway they seem closer than they were for a while. At least they've been together more the last few days."

She made no reference to the wire incident, and

Gretchen sat frowning, staring at the phone after she had hung up. Strange, the girls must not have mentioned it at home. And Sheila especially had been so shaken by it. But then, they had been so busy arguing about Jimmy's car being in the garage that nothing else had seemed important to them.

When Mrs. Carlson honked for her Friday noon, Gretchen locked the door behind her and looked carefully up and down the street before going out to the car. She felt silly doing it and hoped Mrs. Carlson hadn't noticed. But David had been so insistent that she watched every step, she wanted to be able to tell him that she had been careful.

Mrs. Carlson smiled at her as she slid into the car. "You look so cool—like a frosted limeade."

"Unless your church is air conditioned, I'll look and feel like wilted lettuce pretty soon."

"It isn't air conditioned, but it's one of those big old buildings, and we'll be downstairs where it's always cool."

As they pulled to a stop in front of the brick building with ivy climbing over the age-darkened walls, Gretchen looked up at the steeple appreciatively.

"Now if I were interested in church, this is the kind I would go to. It gives a feeling of—of—oh, stability I guess is the word."

She could feel Mrs. Carlson's surprised glance. "You think the appearance of the building makes a difference? That our other one gives a sense of impermanence, brashness even?"

"Yes. That's it exactly." Gretchen felt herself startled in return. She hadn't expected such perception.

She had thought of Mrs. Carlson as being very provincial, with all her attention centered narrowly on her church and family.

After a moment Mrs. Carlson answered, "It depends on what you think the church is. It's not the building that makes the church, you know."

Gretchen didn't, but wanted no discussion that might lead to talk about the beliefs David had tried to share with her last night. She shut her mind sharply now to the memory of what he had tried to say about God and about believing what the Bible said about Him, and his concern to find the truth about Christ. So she said merely, "Of course," in a voice that flatly closed off further comments.

She followed Mrs. Carlson into the church, not surprised to find that she was responsible for the luncheon plans and so was seated at the main table. Sitting with her gave Gretchen a chance to observe the other tables, and she was surprised not only at the large number of women who were there but at the varying degrees of wealth that were evident.

The friendly hum of conversations around the room carried through the luncheon. Gretchen, seated next to Mrs. Carlson near the end of the table, was glad there was no one on the other side to bother her with questions that would require answers. She was there merely as an observer, and as such she watched as the soloist was introduced. She was tall, graceful, not particularly pretty, but with a vivacious face that sparkled even when she was not smiling.

She really knows how to use makeup to the best advantage. Gretchen thought cynically. But she had

116

to admit later, as she watched and listened to the program, that at least some of her radiance came from within. She let the thought cross her mind with reluctance, knowing she didn't want to admit that there really was any difference between people who went to church and talked about it all the time, and people who didn't.

The numbers the soloist sang were completely unfamiliar to Gretchen, some apparently old favorites, others contemporary, and some with melodies that Gretchen thought could have almost any type of words put to them. The musical numbers were interspersed occasionally with talk of the singer's personal faith in Jesus Christ. She spoke of it with no maudlin sentimentality, so Gretchen found she could listen without being embarrassed. But she found she could also listen without being emotionally stirred. So the singer had found what she wanted in Jesus Christ, and that was fine. Not everyone did—she didn't—and she should be allowed that privilege without being preached at.

As she listened, Gretchen let her mind slip back reluctantly to David's words last night when he had talked about believing God's Word and finding life in Jesus Christ. She closed her eyes momentarily in pain at the thought of anything coming between them and made herself concentrate again on the music, only to be haunted by the last lines of one of the songs:

> He comes to thee all unaware
> And makes thee own His loving care.

He has *come unaware*, she thought grimly. *But He isn't wanted!* As she thought the words, her mind answered with the insistent refrain, *David wants Him. David wants Him.*

She had been listening until this moment in a detached, remote way. The unknown dangers that had seemed to lurk around every corner the last few days had gradually begun to fade in the sunshine and warmth of the beautiful summer day and in the company of these friendly women who talked so easily about God as a Friend. Evil had seemed remote. But now, with this song, God Himself seemed to become dangerous.

What tender care had she known before David had come to her? And now God was coming between them. She stirred restlessly, glad when the program was over and she had said polite good-byes to several who spoke to her, avoiding any direct conversation with the singer.

She walked to the car with Mrs. Carlson, listening in silence to her bubbling enthusiasm. "I just wish the girls could have heard her," she finished regretfully. "She has such a contagious personality, and it's so evident that she believes what she sings."

Gretchen stirred impatiently and blurted out, "How much do kids these days believe all that?"

The answer was so long in coming that she half turned to see Mrs. Carlson staring at the road, her forehead wrinkled in thought. Finally she said slowly, "A majority don't believe it at all, I'm afraid. It depends to some extent on how they were raised—"

"You mean, if they were brought up as children to swallow it, they go on forever accepting it as fact, even when they know better?"

"You make it sound like a fairy story, and it's not! I believed as a child and have never had any reason to change my views about God—except to learn more about Him and come to love Him more because of all He has done for me."

"It seems to me you would have to be a child to accept it. It's all too fantastic for an adult to believe."

"Oh, no!" Mrs. Carlson exclaimed.

Gretchen broke in hastily to ward off the lecture she had unconsciously asked for and to keep from remembering that David was not finding it at all fantastic. "We were talking about young people today. You can't judge them all by yours."

"No, that's true, though probably no parent can be entirely sure of his children—of what they are thinking. Ours were raised in the church, and both of them came to a belief in Christ when they were quite young. That in itself gives them a measure of protection from—oh, all that goes on in the world, from its evil."

Gretchen looked away to keep Mrs. Carlson from seeing the beginning of laughter in her eyes. She had no doubt that the church stressed certain moral values, but that didn't necessarily mean that they took with everyone or that only church-oriented people had them. Neither she nor David smoked or drank, and yet she had worked with people who did both—and worse—and still went to church every Sunday. And she could hear again Aunt Phyl's acid comments about the manager in her office who was a Sunday school worker and had deserted his wife and children for another woman, also a church member. *Church didn't put an automatic hedge around anyone*, she thought cynically, though she was sure Mrs. Carlson would never believe that.

She listened again as Mrs. Carlson went on thinking out loud, her eyes on the road but her mind intent on what she was saying.

"There are so many, many temptations these days to the young—to the popular and the unpopular. Drugs, unlimited freedom from any restraint, so many influences to pull them in different directions, away from their childhood training, away from their parents' ideas and beliefs—"

Gretchen shifted impatiently. "No young person in *any* age wants his parents' ideas pushed on him. Everyone wants to think for himself."

"But if the parents' ideas are right—"

Gretchen heard the troubled question in her voice and was sure now that she was speaking personally.

"We have surrounded Sheila and Debra with Christian influences from the time they were born, but even that wouldn't be enough. They had to make a decision for themselves and make their own commitment to Christ so that it became their own personal belief and not just a copy of ours. But even then—"

She stopped and glanced at Gretchen. "I have to be honest with you. This is where the trouble comes. In relating belief to life, I mean. It's hard for any of us to consistently live what we believe, and it's especially hard for young people who are so influenced by their peers. What their friends think is so terribly important to the young, and if their friends don't share their beliefs—"

She left the sentence dangling and then finished in

120

a troubled voice, "There is so much evil abroad in the world."

The word touched Gretchen with cold fingers. She knew; she had felt it. But to believe that a vague faith in a mythical god would ward off the evil, was ridiculous. She couldn't check her quick, impatient, "What I find so impossible to understand is this trying to make real a belief in a remote being off somewhere who actually doesn't exist, who's just an idea someone thought of as a way of escape to blame everything on—"

Mrs. Carlson's breathless, anguished, "Oh, my dear, no!" went unheeded as Gretchen rushed on.

"Look at the mess we're in, the migrants and back-hill people with their horrible living conditions, the blacks and poor whites in the ghettoes, the kids on drugs, war and its victims. All of these people need practical help like money, or better living conditions, or education, or help in coping with life. And they need it right now, not in some far-off imaginary eternal bliss."

She thought then of Ruth and of the anxieties that were eating her and driving her to find escape in drink.

"And look at the poor family whose little boy was kidnapped and killed. What good does it do to tell his parents not to grieve, that everything will work out somehow, that God had a reason for letting it happen? What possible reason could there be for a terrible thing like that? God isn't good—if He does exist—to have a reason for something so horrible."

The car had turned onto her street and pulled to a

stop in front of the house as she talked. Mrs. Carlson leaned over to turn off the ignition before she faced Gretchen.

"I should be able to give you reasons in one-two-three order, but I can't—perhaps because I've never known any of the kinds of trouble you've been talking about. I've never been a member of a minority group—except that every Christian is a minority member in this world. I've never been poor or hungry or despised or had any tragedy happen in my family. Life has always had a glow for me."

She stopped, her eyes still shadowed and now uneasy. "Perhaps I need some hard experiences to make me more understanding of other people and their problems. All I can say is that I believe in God. And I believe that everyone needs to know Jesus Christ as his Saviour, not just for the future, but right now in order to have help to meet trouble if it comes."

"I'm sorry," Gretchen replied, "but I think that is just fantastically unrealistic. If you are a strong person, you'll take the troubles; if you're not, you'll go under." She wanted to add, "I know what I'm talking about. I've got trouble, and it isn't going to do me one bit of good to believe in a make-believe God."

Mrs. Carlson shook her head, the troubled expression still on her face, but her answer was an obstinate "I can't prove it to you by facts. It's too personal a thing. You can only know God's presence by faith."

Gretchen shivered. "That's too mystical for me. It's spooky." She picked up her bag and gloves and reached to open the door, ignoring Mrs. Carlson's protesting "It's not mystical. God is real!"

In spite of her eagerness to escape, she didn't want to be rude and stopped before getting out to say, "Thanks for inviting me. The music was pretty, even if the words were strange." She hesitated and then added, "I don't mean to sound hard. As you said, everyone's attitude is colored by his growing-up experiences. Mine didn't include God when I was young, so He isn't in the picture now."

"It's never too late to include Him," Mrs. Carlson began.

But Gretchen shook her head, pushed open the door, got out, and then stopped to lean down with another quick, "Thanks again."

Mrs. Carlson leaned across the seat to look up at her. "Will we see you Sunday?"

"No! Maybe—I don't know. It depends on whether David—" She couldn't finish. It was no use. David would go. The Bible was getting to him—changing him.

Mrs. Carlson broke into her momentarily brooding thoughts with a laugh. "By the way, poor Sheila has been frantic the last couple of days and has plastered herself with lotion. She hasn't been able to go swimming, and she's absolutely miserable. Poor darling."

"What's the matter?"

"She's allergic to milk. Always has been. The least little bit makes her break out in a rash. Sometimes just being near milk seems to cause the rash. We even had to give her goat's milk when she was a baby."

Gretchen frowned. "That's too bad. I'm afraid I'm responsible for it. She had some while she was over the other night."

Mrs. Carlson nodded. "That's what she said. But it was her fault, so don't blame yourself. She said she felt so bad when she found she'd wakened you, and she got so flustered when you came out to the kitchen that she just grabbed at the first thing in the refrigerator. Then she was too embarrassed to put it back and get something else." She shook her head with a slight frown creasing between her eyes. "I'm afraid she's going to have to learn the hard way to leave things alone that aren't good for her."

Gretchen waved a good-bye and walked up to the house, her mind turning over Mrs. Carlson's last remark. She wondered if there were a double meaning intended unconsciously, remembering again the Carlsons' lack of enthusiasm for Jimmy.

"I wonder if he's the one who's always hanging around her in church?" she mused. "If we go Sunday, I'll ask Mrs. Carlson to point him out."

She stopped to pick a bunch of daisies for the squat yellow vase on the kitchen windowsill and found herself humming. The afternoon had been good for her in spite of what she had had to listen to, she decided. It had lifted a little of the fear and tension that had clouded the week, even though some of Mrs. Carlson's remarks had irritated her. She unlocked the door and went in, pulling the mail out of the box and leafing through it. She made a face in disgust. Mostly bills! They could wait until she took care of the flowers and got into something cooler.

When she finally sat down with a cold drink, she tore open first the envelopes with the boxed windows. Then she picked up the plain white envelope that had no return address, opened it idly, and shook out the slips of paper. At first she thought it was some kind of an advertising gimmick until she arranged the slips in numbered order on the couch beside her and stared at the message.

1. There 2. won't 3. be 4. any 5. more 6. warnings.

It was crazy! She read the words again. Then with one swift motion she stood up and reached to put the snap lock on the screen door. She quickly pushed the inside door shut and locked it, leaning against it with her hands pressed against her trembling mouth. She picked up the envelope and stared at the typewritten address and the postmark. There was nothing to indicate who had sent it. She dropped it on the couch and rubbed her hands down her sides, feeling the clamminess of her palms. She looked at the clock and then ran to the phone, dialing David's office frantically.

"Hello, may I speak to Mr. Marshall, please?" She tried to control the trembling of her voice when she spoke to his secretary, but when David came on the line, her voice was shaking so badly she could hardly stammer out, "David! Oh, David, I'm so frightened!"

"What's the matter?"

"A letter. I got a letter. In the mail. Just now when I got home. It's a warning!"

"Gretchen, wait a minute." His voice was calm and reassuring. "Do you have the doors locked?"

"Yes, yes. Both of them. And the screens too."

"All right. Now, what does the letter say?"

She repeated the words and he asked, "Is that all?"

"Yes."

"Nothing to let you know who sent it?"

125

His calm voice was beginning to quiet her, and she swallowed and answered, "No, just that the postmark is from here in town. And it was mailed yesterday."

"All right, now listen carefully. I'm coming home, but I can't get away for at least a half-hour. I want you to hang up in a minute and call Ruth. Ask her if you can come over and stay with her, and then call me back and let me know. Be careful when you go out. If you see anything that looks the least bit suspicious, go back in and lock the doors. When you get over to Ruth's, call me again. Let her know you are calling me, but don't let her know why," he cautioned.

"David! You don't think that she—"

"I don't think anything yet for sure," he answered. "But we can't take a chance with anyone. We can't trust anyone for sure. When you call me, ask me to bring something home—what, ice cream, maybe? No, we could get that at the drugstore. Anyway, it would melt. Flowers—that's it, tell me you'd like me to bring some flowers. And then I'll tell you I'm coming home early, and you act surprised."

"David, I'm so nervous, I'm afraid I'll give everything away, just by my voice."

His voice was grim as he answered, "Just remember that you are trying to protect your own life. I'll wait to hear from you. And Gretchen—"

"Yes?"

"I don't know if I have any right to ask God for help, but I'm going to do it anyway."

Gretchen was crying. "David, please! I know that's supposed to help, but it doesn't. It just makes me more frightened."

126

"Don't let it, darling. Think of me then. I love you. Be careful when you go out. I'll be following you with my mind every minute."

She nodded, whispering back, "I love you too. I'll be careful. But hurry, David. Hurry home. I need you!"

She followed his directions and called Ruth, who answered, "Yes, *please* come over and stay as long as you can because I'm dying for some adult company, and I've been wondering where you were since there was no answer when I called you a little while ago."

After calling David back, Gretchen went to the back door and looked out. No one was in sight as she unlocked the door and stepped out onto the porch, keeping one hand on the open screen door as she looked around. But the memory of the wire across the driveway forced her back inside, and she closed and locked the door again. It would be better anyway to go out the front door and along the sidewalk where there would be people she could call out to if necessary, rather than to cut across deserted backyards where anyone could be hiding. She walked through the house, feeling its silence, and unlocked the front door, pulling it open cautiously.

She looked along the street in each direction. A car went by with children hanging out all the windows shrieking at one another. Another car, empty, stood in front of the house on the corner. The three Benson children were noisy with laughter as they poured water over each other in the plastic wading pool in their driveway. She could see Mr. Graves' spare figure bent over his rosebushes.

127

The sun reflected on all the windows of the houses across the street, lighting them and leaving no dark shadows anywhere. The rapid beating of the pulse in her throat gradually stilled. The thought of danger and evil was out of place in the quiet peace of the familiar neighborhood. She closed the door quickly, hearing the firm click of the lock behind her, and hurried down to the sidewalk and along it to Ruth's. David would be wondering why she was so long in calling back. The front door was standing open, and Gretchen hurried inside, fighting down the impulse to close and lock it behind her.

"How can you bear to rush so fast on such a hot day?" Ruth looked up at her from where she sat on the floor, helping Brian build a tower of blocks.

"It's cooled off some," Gretchen answered absently. As she watched Ruth's slender figure and saw her laughing at Brian, she felt guilty at the moment of doubt she'd had about her. But she had to let Ruth know she was calling David so he would know where she was. In fact, as she went toward the phone in response to Ruth's "Help yourself," she decided to tell Ruth about the letter, and maybe about the other things that had happened too. It might be good for her to know that other people had problems that were real rather than imaginary.

She dialed David's number and waited for the connection, leaning back against the wall as she glanced into the small den off the kitchen that Ruth called her "escape hatch." She smiled to herself at how well it mirrored Ruth's personality. The typewriter sat precisely in the middle of the desk, typing paper was neatly lined along one side, the stack of envelopes was arranged in an orderly pile.

Then her fingers tightened convulsively on the phone as the significance of what she was seeing hit her. Plain envelopes. White envelopes. Envelopes just like the one she had opened such a short time ago.

She couldn't control her voice enough to reply when David answered and it took his sharp, "Gretchen! Is everything all right?" to bring her alert. She had to remember she was playing a part in what could be a deadly performance. So, in what she hoped was a normal voice, she said clearly, "David? Hi. I'm at Ruth's. Look, I've got a sudden yen to have some fresh flowers tonight."

How dumb! she realized then. *Ruth knows we've got a yard full of flowers.* She said quickly, "I mean a corsage—I haven't had one for a long time. Do I have to have a reason? Well, let's say to celebrate the fact that we've been married eight months, three weeks, and two days. . . . You remembered too? Can you come home a little early, do you think?. . . . Good. . . . Yes, I'm at Ruth's. . . . I'll stay right here until you come."

Her mouth said the words, while her mind was trying desperately to figure a way out. If she sat down beside Brian in the living room and played with him, she would surely be safe. Ruth wouldn't attempt anything in front of him. She put the phone down slowly and watched as Ruth stood up and came toward her, smiling.

"I called David," she said, hearing her unnaturally loud voice. And then she repeated, "I told David I was with you. He knows I'm here."

Ruth laughed. "I heard you the first time." Then her glance shifted beyond Gretchen into the den and back at her again. Her eyes narrowed and she moved swiftly, suddenly, to pull the door of the den shut and then turned to stand with her back to it defiantly.

"Well?" she glared.

Gretchen licked at her dry lips. "Well what?"

"So you saw."

"No. I didn't. I don't know what you mean."

"Don't you dare tell Jack!"

"Jack?" Gretchen's mind echoed. How could he help not knowing eventually if Ruth went through with whatever plan she had?

Aloud she asked, "Why not?" thinking she could play for time. Someone might come to the door —David might get home in time. She backed away as Ruth moved toward her, a fixed, white look on her face.

"Because he would hate it if he found out, and I'm only doing it to help him, but he won't see it that way, and he'll say I shouldn't have done it because he's so proud and independent and he thinks women should be the helpless, clinging-vine type. I'd like to be like that but I have to think of our future too. And what will happen to Brian and me if something happens to Jack?"

Gretchen retreated until her knees hit against a chair as she stared at Ruth. "What are you talking about?"

Ruth gestured back at the closed den door. "That! Didn't you see? I know you did. The typewriter, I mean, and all those envelopes that I'm addressing to send out for this agency, and I have to do three hundred a day to fill my quota and get the top pay, but at least I have to stay s-sober to do it, so I guess it's worth it."

She grabbed Brian as he got up from his blocks and came to stand beside her anxiously, his "Mommy cry?" this time a question as he looked up into her face.

Gretchen sank down into the chair, weak with relief, not knowing whether to laugh or cry or scold herself. To have suspected Ruth!

"I won't tell Jack," she promised. "But how long have you been doing this?"

"Just this week. I'd seen an ad quite a while ago and thought about applying, but when you found me the other day was what decided me, because I knew I *had* to do something about myself."

She sat down on the floor beside Brian again, aimlessly piling blocks which he solemnly scattered. She looked up at Gretchen obliquely.

"You see—I've always had this—this problem, about drinking, I mean. Jack knew, and he said he didn't care and that he was sure I'd get over it because there wasn't any reason to drink if a person was happy. And I *was* happy, and for a long time after we were married everything was all right because there wasn't anything that I needed to escape from because Jack was so sweet and wonderful, and then when Brian came, that was all the more reason not to, and I didn't want to, I really didn't."

She stopped and then went on with a helpless gesture that grabbed at Gretchen.

"But now when things have been so scary the last few months, and Jack is all uptight over all the crime, and there are so many people all over doing such awful things, even teenagers with their drugs, and people having babies when they're not married and bragging about it, and then this little boy got killed for no reason at all, and they'll never find the ones who did it, so they could even go on doing it over and over—"

Her voice trailed off to a ragged edge, and Gretchen sat helplessly watching the tears slide down her cheeks. How could she ever have thought to tell Ruth about the letter and bring her terror so close to home!

And now what could she say or do to help? Fragments of words, isolated phrases that had been said at the luncheon, came back to her. Some of David's quotes from the Bible, things Mrs. Carlson had said, sentences she had thought she had only half heard from the minister's sermons, flooded her mind. She didn't believe them, but she could at least repeat them. They might help Ruth.

So she tried. "Some people think—God—helps when they are in trouble." She heard David's voice as she spoke when he said, "I'm praying," and her mind answered him now silently, *Don't you see that doesn't help when I don't believe there is a God to pray to?*

And she listened as Ruth said scornfully, "I don't believe in God. I've never had any help from Him, have you?" She looked up at Gretchen, her intense face demanding an answer.

She shook her head wordlessly, letting herself remember how desperately she had prayed for God to intervene that day she had come home from school to find the house empty and her parents gone without a word. He hadn't helped, for sending her to dour Aunt Phyl had been no answer.

"But there are some people who seem to believe in Him," she went on. "I don't know—they say it really works."

"They say," Ruth blazed. "What do *they* know in their safe little world when they thank their God for their security and it's my husband who is out there keeping them safe, not God. Even you don't understand. How can I tell you about my dread when the phone rings or someone comes to the door while Jack is gone and I wonder if it's the chief coming to tell me—to tell me—" After a moment, in a voice thick with tears, she said, "You don't have any idea what it's like to be scared, I mean *really* scared."

Gretchen was silent. She wanted to say, "But I do know!" and knew she couldn't add her terror to Ruth's burden of fear.

"Everyone has his own secret fears, I guess," she said then slowly. "And if some people find that God helps—well," she smiled at Ruth faintly. "If that's what they need, OK."

They sat together in silence, each enmeshed in her own fears and anguish, with Brian playing between them. The sun poured in to light and warm the room. *And yet*, Gretchen thought, *the light and warmth isn't even touching us. We're both in a shadowed world of terror—Ruth's no less real than mine—with nowhere to turn for help.*

Illogically she thought of Mrs. Carlson. She claimed to have a refuge from trouble. But she didn't need one. Her world had no secret fears, no unseen dangers.

SIX

DAVID SUGGESTED that they go out to a quiet restaurant for a change of scenery and go over all the events piece by piece, but Gretchen shook her head in panic at the thought.

"No, please, David! Let's stay home. I'd be afraid someone had gotten in while we were gone and—oh, I don't know." She shivered. "Done something. Or planted something. Let's have dinner at home. I can wear my corsage here just as well and enjoy it just as much."

Then as he answered, "All right, darling, if you'd rather," she pleaded, "David, let's move! Let's not stay here. If whoever is doing this wants our house or wants to get rid of us for some reason, let's not fight it. Please?"

He caught her hands and pulled her down on the couch beside him. "Gretchen, listen. We have to trace this somehow and find out who is doing this and why—"

"I don't care who it is! Or why! I just want to feel safe again!"

"We have to find out. If whoever it is succeeds with us, he might turn on someone else. Don't you see?"

She nodded, forcing back tears. "I suppose you're right," she whispered.

"I think we'll have to go to the police and get help."

"Can we do it without Jack finding out? If Ruth knows there is danger right here in the neighborhood, she'll go all to pieces. I know she will. She's on the edge of panic every day."

He gnawed his lip, a worried frown lining furrows across his forehead.

"I suppose it can be kept from him. I don't know enough about police files and so on to know how they handle these things. Though with Jack right here on the block, he would be the logical one to be put on the case. He might know something about the people in the neighborhood that we don't, since he's lived here longer. But he wouldn't tell Ruth. You know he wouldn't do anything to frighten or upset her."

She looked at him with a puzzled frown while her mind caught at his words. "What do you mean he might know something about the neighborhood? We've already gone over everyone on the block and decided it couldn't be any of the neighbors. They don't know us and we don't know them."

"Don't you see that it's the fact that we *don't* know them that might be the clue? Maybe someone has a quirk that we don't know about."

"What about the letter?" she asked suddenly. "Can they trace typewriters?"

"Yes, but where can they start? The police can't just go from door to door and demand a sample from everyone who has a typewriter. Oh, I suppose they could get search warrants but—'' He broke off in frustration.

A vision of Ruth's typewriter swam before her, and she found herself thinking again that it *could* be Ruth, even though she knew in her heart that it wasn't.

She watched David as he walked back and forth through the living room, thinking out loud. "We must be overlooking some vital point, some very obvious clue that's right there and we can't see it. There must be *something* someone said or did that is important and we didn't catch it at the time."

"This is where my supposed photographic mind would come in handy," she said with a faint attempt at humor. Then she frowned as she heard her words. She had a vague feeling that something Mrs. Carlson had said at some time was important. Something she had said one day had started a train of thought. *And I didn't follow it at the time*, she scolded herself. Now it was gone.

"It might help to make a list of everything that has happened," David suggested. "When the first phone call came, the time, anything you can remember about the atmosphere, how the breathing sounded—anything that might give the police a clue to go on. We can't go to them with just a vague story of fright." He looked at her then, his mouth grim. "Though the wire and the letter are certainly not vague."

He got pen and paper and sat down beside her. "Has anyone different walked by the house or come to the door in the last few weeks? Say, a magazine salesman or a repairman?"

137

She shook her head. "Not since the phone calls started."

"Before that though. The week before."

"No."

"Did you talk to anyone outside that you didn't know? Like someone visiting next door?"

"No."

"Has there been any car, different from the usual ones on the block, that you remember seeing?"

She gestured futilely. "David, when I'm weeding or—or even sitting outside reading, I don't look at every car or even every person who goes by!"

He frowned down at the blank paper in his hand. "Well, let's try to put down the time sequence anyway, and that will give us a start. When did the first phone call come? It was late, wasn't it?"

She thought back, suddenly surprised to find that it had all started only two weeks ago. "On Friday," she said. "I remember because it was the night the minister was here. It was hot, and you were showering, and I was afraid it was bad news from your parents." She watched as he jotted down the date and then the others as she remembered them.

Friday, June 12—first call (late night)
Monday, June 15—second and third calls (late afternoon)
Tuesday, June 16—three calls (afternoon)
Wednesday, June 17—four calls (afternoon)
Thursday, June 18—three calls (afternoon)
Friday, June 19—three calls (afternoon)
Monday, June 22—movement in bushes (late night)

Wednesday, June 24—wire across driveway (early morning)

Friday, June 26—letter in mail

They looked at the list. "It's not much, is it?" Gretchen asked forlornly.

"One thing seems clear," David said finally. "It all seems definitely aimed at you. Except for the first call, all the rest came when you would naturally be home alone. And I wasn't here for the other things either, though I don't know how the person, whoever it is, would know that." He looked at her urgently. "Think carefully, Gretchen. Are there any people, any person at all, who may be connected with any of these incidents? Had you seen or talked to any one person before each of the calls, for instance?"

She studied the list, trying to think back. "Well, you were here when the first call came. Ruth was here when one came on the sixteenth. Mrs. Carlson stopped in on Friday, and one came while she was here. The twins were here the morning we found the wire—thankfully. If they hadn't been, I'd be sitting here with my leg in a cast—or worse." She looked at the list again and shook her head. "There's just no connection with anyone. Whoever is doing this is a complete stranger who just happened to pick us. I'm convinced of that. There just isn't any other explanation."

David shook his head obstinately. "There *has* to be a connection. Either that, or these are absolutely unrelated events that just accidentally happened at the same time. And that's impossible."

139

He frowned down at the list again and then said slowly, "You see, things are getting worse all the time. We don't know what this letter means, but we have to believe that whoever sent it means what he says. He—she—began with fairly harmless phone calls and has gone on getting progressively more serious."

He looked at her soberly, and Gretchen stared back. She felt again the panic that had gripped her that afternoon as she had stared at the typed message and felt there was no place where she would be secure.

"David, I'm frightened," she whispered.

He put his arm around her protectively but his words were not comforting as he answered, "So am I. Frightened and baffled."

"What are we going to do?"

"I'm going to the police station tomorrow. But I think we have to be very careful. We must assume, even though we don't know why, that all of this has been deliberately planned against you, against us, instead of being intended for someone else. In that case, we have to assume that the someone—whoever it is—may be nearby, may be in a position to watch everything we do, and is aware of where you go and what you do at any hour of the day. That's why I come back to thinking it must be someone in the neighborhood. So we have to be careful not to get him—or her—suspicious. That's why we can't be seen talking to the police or have a policeman come to the house. I'll—"

"David! I did talk to a policeman! To Jack the day I took care of Brian. He came over to see how Brian was, and he was in his uniform and his patrol car was parked right out in front!"

"Of our house?"

"No, I don't think so—no, I'm sure it wasn't. He came home to see how Ruth was, and he parked there, I'm sure. But then he came over here and we were talking."

"What day was that? After the phone calls stopped?"

"Oh, I don't remember. I can't think! Before maybe—no—I'm not sure if they had even started yet. But that's not the important thing. What worries me is that everyone on the block could have seen us because we stood right outside the house. Jack was talking about Ruth and then about that little boy being killed—David, I'm so afraid! And there isn't anyone we can talk to because we have to suspect everyone."

He was silent. Then he said, "Except one person. There's one person we can trust, I'm sure."

"Who?"

"The minister."

"But we don't know him. We haven't been going to church long enough. He wouldn't want to get mixed up in something like this."

"I think he would." He glanced at the clock. "It's not late. I'm going to call him."

"David." She stood up and followed him to the phone. "David. The trouble is—well—you—you know I don't believe anything."

"I don't think that will matter to him. All he will think about is that you need help."

"But I mean—" She was desperate to make herself

141

clear. "You see—I—I can't expect God to help me when I haven't needed Him before—when I haven't even thought He *was*."

He considered that for a moment, staring gravely back at her. Finally he cleared his throat.

"I don't know much about it either, darling, but from what I understand, that won't matter. To God, I mean."

She watched him and listened as he dialed, talked briefly, and put down the phone. He came back to her.

"He's on his way over."

"But what can he *do*?"

"I don't know." He walked over to stare out the door into the soft darkness and then turned back to sit down beside her on the couch. "Maybe nothing but pray."

They sat in silence, waiting, David's arm tight around Gretchen's shoulders. She jumped nervously when the car door slammed in the driveway, then relaxed her clenched fists. She stood up when David opened the door, nodded at Mr. Gorman with a faint smile, and then sat down as the two men shook hands.

"We seem to be involved in a strange situation, and we need help from someone outside of it," David began. He sketched the story and showed the list of dates they had worked out and the letter.

Gretchen watched Mr. Gorman's face anxiously with the foolish hope that he would have a magic answer. The hope faded when he said seriously, "I don't think you should waste any more time. I'd get to the police with this the first thing in the morning. Or even tonight yet. It may only be someone's idea of a joke, but you can't be sure."

"We were afraid doing that might precipitate more trouble."

He shook his head. "If this turns out to be just a crank, the police have the best chance of tracing it. If it's serious, the police are still the best ones to deal with it. They can put an inconspicuous guard on the house and have police cars here in a few moments' time if necessary."

"One of our neighbors is a policeman," David began.

He considered it a moment and then shook his head. "Go directly to the station. That way it will be official even though he may be the one assigned to the case."

David nodded. "Thanks. That had been my thinking, but I needed confirmation."

Mr. Gorman looked at them thoughtfully. "I hope you are considering another source of help?"

Hope sprang in Gretchen. "Who?" But as she asked she knew what his answer would be, and she sank back against the cushions on the couch, dreading to hear it.

"God."

David cleared his throat, staring at his hands as he gripped them together. He said slowly, "Our problem is that we haven't felt any need of God before now. It doesn't seem right—I mean—well, the fact is we haven't any—any claim on Him."

Mr. Gorman interrupted, shaking his head. "No one has a claim on God, a right to His goodness and mercy.

The Bible says He sends the rain on the just and the unjust. You can look around and see that for yourself."

David didn't look up as he asked, "But isn't there a difference? You said something once about those who belong to God as His children and those who don't. I've been—I've been reading the Bible—I know there is a difference—"

"Yes, that's true. Everyone belongs to God in the sense that God created all men. But some people are His children in a special way since they belong to Him because of their faith in Jesus Christ. When you have children of your own you'll understand this better. I love the kids in the church, and when they come to me for help of some kind, I give it if I can. But my own?" He laughed. "That's something else again. They're mine. They belong to me, and I'd do anything for them."

"So we can—ask God to help us now even though we don't—belong to Him—yet? In the way you mean? In the way He wants?"

David asked his questions haltingly, longingly, and all his searching lay plainly on his face. Gretchen looked at him through eyes brimming with tears.

Dear David! she thought. *How transparent he is in his wanting God. I'll never object again to going to church. If he wants God this much, I'll never stop him. If I can't believe, I can pretend for him.*

Mr. Gorman was smiling back at David and nodding his head. "Let's ask Him now." He bowed his head and prayed so simply and so intimately that Gretchen was sure if she opened her eyes she would see God standing there. It was not altogether a comforting feeling, and she was glad to raise her head to the familiar room without an alien presence.

Mr. Gorman stood up. "If I can do anything more, let me know." He looked at Gretchen. "You'll want to be careful. Don't go anyplace alone until you get some directions from the police. Maybe you ought to go away somewhere." He looked questioningly from one to the other.

David shook his head. "No. That wouldn't get us to the bottom of this. We've got to clear it up if there is any answer to the puzzle." He put his arm around Gretchen. "I'll go to the police the first thing in the morning and then stay home the rest of the day. Then we'll take it from there and make plans as we can, depending on what the police discover."

Gretchen supposed it was superstition to think that it was Mr. Gorman's prayer that made her sleep that night, but she did, more soundly than she had for the last two weeks. She was surprised to waken to the smell of coffee and frying bacon and went out to the kitchen rubbing her eyes.

"Morning, sweetheart." David kissed the top of her head and put a hand under her chin to lift her face and look down at her lovingly. He ran a finger lightly across each cheek under her eyes. "I'm glad to see the dark shadows have faded a little. Last night you looked like an elf who'd lost her reason for living."

She rose on tiptoe to give him a kiss. "Last night I was tired and scared."

"And now?"

"I'm not tired. And I'm not *as* scared. I'm afraid I'm

pretty much of a pagan, because I always feel better when it's light. The dark is scary!" She shivered and then sniffed. "The coffee smells better than it does when I make it," she said jealously and poured a cup. "Umm, good! You can do it every morning."

He put down the pancake turner he was holding, carefully lowered the heat under the griddle, and turned to her gravely.

"I'm suddenly realizing how precious you are to me. To have you threatened—to face having you harmed—" He broke off, his voice rough, and put his arms around her protectively. "If we ever find the person who is doing this, he'll be sorry."

After a moment she said, "David?"

"Umm?"

"What if—what if there isn't a God to help?"

"The Bible says there is." He spoke with such simplicity and faith that she was sure he had capitulated. He had gone ahead and left her behind in the darkness of uncertainty.

She felt his arms tighten around her and heard the urgency in his voice as he said, "Gretchen, you said once to let you know if I found something in the Bible by a woman. I have."

She waited tensely.

He quoted softly, "'Whither thou goest, I will go; and where thou lodgest, I will lodge: thy people shall be my people, and thy God my God.'* Would you—if I find God, will you have Him too?"

"I don't know," she managed to say finally in a voice choked with held-back tears.

*Ruth 1:16.

146

They ate breakfast, pretending a gaiety neither felt. After David had gone, making sure before he left that the doors were securely locked, she washed the dishes and vacuumed the rugs. If the police came to talk to her, she wanted the house to be spotless. And she had to keep busy so she wouldn't think of David's question.

He had said he didn't know how long he would be and she was just to wait in the house until he came back or called. To fill the time, she wrote a letter to his parents, feeling guilty that it had been so long since she had written—not since, she realized, the calls had begun to come. They would be wondering what was wrong. It was difficult to think of chatty, inconsequential things to talk about with her mind ceaselessly asking Why? and Who? She finally managed, by writing big, to fill two pages.

She walked through the house restlessly, thinking again of captive animals, and then thinking of David who was moving into a world of faith that was foreign to her. She went to the front door and pulled it open to look out on the quiet street. David had only been gone a little more than half an hour. How time dragged when one waited!

She looked down the length of the street to the mailbox on the corner. It wouldn't hurt at all to run down and mail the letter. That wouldn't be like going anywhere, which David had said she mustn't do. She would still be in sight of the house. She got the letter and stepped out, looking in both directions. The street was the same as always, with children's voices laughing and the sounds of music and play. The brightness of the day erased the fears that had come with last night's darkness.

The mailbox beckoned to her as she stood on the front steps. To get to it she had only to pass the house next door where Mixie lay lazily in the shade of the tree in the middle of the lawn, and walk past Ruth's house where the front door would be quickly opened if she needed an emergency refuge, and then go along beside the beautiful corner lot of the house that faced on the other street. There were no bushes, no shrubbery, absolutely no place where someone could jump out at her unexpectedly. Nothing dangerous could possibly happen to her in the middle of the bright sunny morning on a pleasant, tree-shaded street of nice people—and within sight of her own house.

With a light step she walked down the two front steps from the porch; along the walk to the main sidewalk; and passed Mixie, who didn't even lift his head, though his tail showed signs of life momentarily. She looked at Ruth's house as she walked by and imagined her hard at work addressing her three hundred envelopes. The pathos of it clutched at her and she thought, *Maybe when this is all over I can help her. Maybe I can be more of a neighbor to her and help her overcome her fears.*

She was so engrossed in her plans for the future that a car slid quietly to the curb beside her before she was aware of it. She looked over, startled, and then relieved to see Sheila's laughing face.

"Hi, Mrs. Marshall! Can we give you a lift?"

Gretchen smiled and walked over to the car.

"Thanks, but I'm just going to the corner to the mailbox."

She looked down at Sheila's bright face turned up toward her and then at the boy behind the wheel.

"So this is the elusive Jimmy," she smiled. "I wondered when I was going to meet you."

She smiled down at them as they sat close together. Sheila's long blond hair, tangled by the wind, lay partly over Jimmy's shoulder as she sat pressed against him. Instead of the clean, well-tailored slacks or the shorts or crisp cotton dresses Gretchen had usually seen her wearing, Sheila was dressed like Jimmy in dirty blue jeans and matching shirts, with wide, studded cowboy belts. Neither one was wearing shoes.

They should have on cowboy boots, some insistent memory whispered, and she looked at the back seat of the convertible which was a jumble of blankets and towels and bathing suits.

And Gretchen knew where she had seen them before and fought to keep the knowledge from showing in her eyes. The only difference was that there were no dark red splotches on Sheila's arm today. The rash had covered her arm that day they had stopped beside her for the traffic light, and she had been so revolted by the quick glimpse she had had of their necking that she had kept from looking at them. But she had seen enough, and they must have thought she had seen more, for she remembered now that there had been a baby bottle showing at one corner of the cardboard box that had been on the back seat that day.

The sickening thing hit her with terrifying force

149

and paralyzed her as she stared down at Sheila. She didn't know how it could be—she didn't know why she was so sure. But it was true! They were the ones—Sheila and Jimmy—who had kidnapped the little boy. But that meant they had killed him, too.

She tried to cover her knowledge and moved to back away. But Sheila was too quick for her as she lunged suddenly and grabbed Gretchen's wrist with steel fingers.

"Get in!" She spit the words in a voice Gretchen didn't recognize.

She shook her head wordlessly and twisted to pull away from Sheila's grasp. Then she saw the gun Jimmy had pulled from his wide cowboy belt and held flat against his stomach, pointing at her.

"Do as she says," he ordered, his voice hard. "Don't make any noise. Make it look natural."

Gretchen gave a desperate look around as Sheila leaned further to push down on the door handle with her other hand without letting go of Gretchen's wrist. There was absolutely no one in sight, and she was sure Jimmy would shoot if she screamed. Held by the steel grip, there was nothing for her to do but get into the car.

The car moved off instantly, picking up speed as it turned the corner. But she noticed that Jimmy was keeping well within the speed limit, not risking being stopped by the police. He took several turns immediately, and she was sure this was to get away from the neighborhood as quickly as possible. She could only hope that David would get home quickly. But even if he did, she knew he would have no clue to begin tracing her. He would never suspect Sheila; no one would. No one had seen her get into the car. And even if someone had, he would not have looked twice at the perfectly normal sight of a woman voluntarily getting into a car with two laughing teenagers. Who would ever think to look at the license number of the car? Or remember it if he did?

The incredibility of the situation overwhelmed her. How *could* it be Sheila? How could a murderer be the girl who stood in church singing hymns in a clear, sweet voice, who sometimes taught a Sunday school class, who smiled at her parents and was obedient to them, who laughed so easily, who sat in her living room and talked about believing in Jesus—

Her thoughts stopped abruptly. This was just a horrible nightmare! They were playing a joke on her! She turned slightly to look at Sheila, hoping desperately to see beside her the clear-eyed, sunny girl she had known the past two weeks. But she found that Jimmy had given Sheila the gun and she was holding it close to her body so that it could not be seen easily. But it was there, and she was holding it casually, with a mocking smile on her face.

As Gretchen met her eyes, Sheila laughed. "Surprised?" she asked gaily.

Gretchen turned her head wordlessly and looked straight ahead. What she had seen in Sheila's eyes gave the answer to the *why* she had been asking. There was something wrong with her.

Sheila's features were the same. There were the clear skin, the heart-shaped face, the slender eyebrows arching over the deep-set blue eyes so like her

151

mother's. But the expression was different—distorted. The expression on her face was excited but at the same time blurred. Gretchen had no doubt that Sheila knew exactly what she was doing, but it was being done through a distorted perspective, a warped mind. She didn't dare look at Jimmy, afraid of what evil she would surely see in his face. She swallowed hard, knowing she was desperately afraid.

"You won't get away with this, you know," she said finally, trying to sound casual and conversational, and amazing herself at how steady her voice sounded. "My husband has the day off and just went out on a quick errand and was coming right back."

Sheila jeered, "Sure, we saw him go. Don't try to kid us. He was going to work. And even if he did come back, how's he going to find you? There wasn't anybody on the street when we picked you up. That was great timing, Jimmy boy. And nice of you to come out all by yourself so we didn't have to come in after you."

Gretchen swallowed again, the fright deepening. "Probably my friend was looking out the window," she went on with her desperate attempt at indifference.

"Naw. She went to the store with her kid. We saw her." Jimmy was chewing gum nonchalantly as he drove carefully through town.

"And you won't get any help from the minister either," Sheila added.

Gretchen jerked her head to look at her. "How did you know—"

"We've been watching you," Jimmy answered the question.

"For two weeks," Sheila added and poked the gun in Gretchen's ribs. "We've been by your house lots of times, and you never saw us," she crowed.

Gretchen closed her eyes and tried to stop the shudder that threatened to convulse her. She didn't have to ask why they'd been watching. All the pieces were falling into place one by one. She saw with terrifying clarity how the trivial, the happenstance, the seeming coincidences, fit the pattern that would lead, she had no doubt, to her death at the hands of these two teenagers who must be high on drugs and the excitement of a kill. Little, unrelated pieces of events whirled together in a kaleidoscope of sharp, horrible colors and fell into place to form the hideous nightmare through which she was living—and would die.

Seeing them that day in the car at the stoplight had meant nothing to her at the time and probably had meant nothing to them either. She was no witness at that time. But then she had suddenly showed up at church and Sheila had recognized her. What next? She frowned, thinking. What had made Sheila wary, suspicious? What had made them decide she was dangerous? What had she done?

Then she remembered. It had been David's remark at the dinner table about her memory. She could see again Sheila's face—flushed, excited, intent—as she had leaned forward asking questions. Gretchen had thought it schoolgirl envy of an easy way to do homework. Instead, Sheila must have been afraid of discovery and had begun cold calculations to silence her. David's remark had probably been the deciding factor. She remembered that Jimmy had come over that afternoon, and they must have begun to lay their plans then. But Debra. Debra was there. Did she know? Was she in on this too?

"Didn't you ever wonder why you never saw Jimmy?" Sheila asked mockingly.

Gretchen could only shake her head, though she knew why now. He hadn't wanted to be seen. But if she had seen him, at church, perhaps, dressed in suit and tie, would she have recognized him? Probably not. She hadn't remembered Sheila in a different setting.

They were the ones who had done it all. The phone calls. And the noise in the bushes. She closed her eyes again, painfully remembering how Sheila had caught her breath in pretended horror and fright when she had heard about it. Remembering too that she had innocently taken into her house the one responsible for the terror. How they must have laughed that night sitting out in the car!

"But the wire?" she asked. "Why did you warn me? You put it there."

Sheila laughed. "To keep you from being suspicious. I *wanted* to let you fall," she pouted, "but Jimmy thought the other way was better."

Jimmy slowed the car and turned off the main road and into a forest-preserve entrance, driving slowly along the narrow path. To Gretchen's blurred sight the surroundings looked like a jungle. He stopped the car finally and got out, coming around to the door on her side.

"Get out!" he ordered with a jerk of his head, and

she obeyed, feeling the gun prodding her in the back.

As she stumbled along the path behind Jimmy with Sheila close at her heels, she had only one thought. *Keep them talking.* she said to herself desperately. *If I can just keep them talking, maybe someone will come in time.*

"When did you put the wire there?"

"While you were sleeping. When Jimmy called, I told him you'd be going out to the garage so it was a perfect setup. And then *you* had to wake up and come out. I didn't think you'd see that tiny light. I just barely had time to get in from the porch and close the back door before you got to the kitchen." She stopped, her lower lip pouting as she remembered the inconvenience.

Gretchen thought then of the click she had heard that night. She had taken for granted it was the sound of the refrigerator door closing when it had been the back door. If she hadn't stopped to turn on a light on the way, she would have seen Sheila coming in. What would have happened to her that night if she had been suspicious then and showed it? She wondered, and shuddered.

She listened numbly as Sheila went on: "I just had time to grab some milk from the refrigerator when you turned on the kitchen light. Even though I managed to spill it so I wouldn't have to drink it, I still got a reaction thanks to you," and she jabbed Gretchen again. "And you thought it spilled accidentally, didn't you?" she demanded gleefully. "I was really clever that time."

As Gretchen nodded wordlessly, Sheila's voice

hardened. "Then dumb old Debra came out, and when she finally got it through her head that I had taken milk, she got suspicious. I had a hard time stopping her questions and really had to talk my way out of that one. I didn't think she'd wake up from the sleeping pills I had put in her coke. But she did, and she almost messed the whole thing up."

Sheila stopped and frowned for a moment. "You know, I think we're going to have to take care of her next."

"Probably," Jimmy answered carelessly over his shoulder.

Gretchen listened in horror and felt the last hope of trying to talk them out of their plans drain away from her. How could *she* expect mercy from them when they had killed a helpless little child and talked so casually of killing a sister? Snatches of phrases came to her out of nowhere as she stumbled along the narrow path after Jimmy, with Sheila at her back constantly prodding her with the gun. They were words she had listened to with distaste when David had read them that day in the airport, but now she held onto them in desperation.

"LORD, thou hast been our dwelling place. . . . There shall no evil befall thee. . . . Thou shalt not be afraid for the terror by night. . . . nor for the destruction that wasteth at noonday. . . . he shall give his angels charge over thee."

O God, she pleaded silently, *please help me! David, find me! Ask God to help you find me!*

But with the plea her thoughts were accusing. Why should she expect God to save her when He had let an innocent, defenseless child be killed by these same mad people? But maybe—maybe that was why she should be saved. The baby was innocent of wrongdoing, but she wasn't. He had never ignored God, disbelieved in Him; but she had. She needed a second chance. She needed to be saved. David was talking about needing to be saved. But he didn't mean this kind. He meant another kind. David! *O God, help me! David, find me! Ask God to help you find me!*

Her thoughts ran on incoherently as she was prodded and pushed along the narrow, winding path deeper into the underbrush. The branches of low trees whipped against her face and tangled in her hair as Jimmy carelessly pushed through, letting them snap back on her. She stumbled and fell, tearing her nylons and cutting her leg so that it bled.

Remembering how Sheila had turned her face away at the sight of the blood on her legs when she had fallen against the wire, Gretchen turned suddenly with some crazy thought of throwing Sheila off balance at the sight of the blood and ducking away out of range of the gun and running for her life. Surely she could lose them in the underbrush and gradually work her way toward the road and stop a passing car.

But Sheila only laughed at her and grabbed her shoulders and pushed her on again. Gretchen went cold with the realization that, instead of its sickening her, Sheila was excited by the sight of blood. She had hidden her face that morning to keep from revealing too much. But Debra had said—Debra seemed to believe— In that moment of renewed fear, Gretchen found time to wonder how much Debra knew about her twin. Surely she must have suspected something about her, unless she was in on this too.

They came out then into a small clearing completely encircled by trees, hidden away from the casual picnicker. Gretchen stared around perplexed, wondering why it seemed familiar. Then she remembered. She had seen it pictured over and over in the newspapers and on television. This was where they had taken the little boy. This was where he had been kept. His body had been found here, and she stared across the clearing at the ground which showed signs of recently turned earth. *But why would they come back here?* she wondered wildly, and shuddered as the answer came. They were confident they were under no suspicion, confident that they would not be discovered.

They backed her roughly up against a tree and stood looking at her.

"Any more questions?" Sheila asked mockingly. Then, without waiting for an answer, she shook her head in mock sorrow. "It's too bad you came to church. Church wasn't a good place for you—not ours anyway. You should have stayed away. That just proves that church isn't for everyone. Church isn't for everyone, not for everyone."

Gretchen stared at her as though hypnotized as she half sang the words over and over, her eyes partly closed as she swayed back and forth in time to the rhythm of the words. She surveyed Gretchen through her narrowed eyes, shaking her head, her long blond hair stringing limply over her shoulders.

Gretchen stared back, wondering where the prettiness and cleanness had gone. Her face seemed bloated and her eyes were glazed. Jimmy stood to one side smoking a cigarette, the acrid burning smell coming faintly to her in the clear air. He was watching Sheila, an amused, indulgent smile on his lips; and Gretchen felt her eyes drawn irresistibly back to the girl's face.

Now Sheila's mood had changed. She was shaking her head sadly and looking as though she were about to cry.

"The folks tried—they tried to make me good—they couldn't see that I didn't want any of the goodness. Oh, I did at first, when I was little. But then it wasn't exciting enough. Something in me needs excitement—danger—and they couldn't see it. They kept giving me a Bible—praying at me—shoving church at me."

She stopped to blink back tears and pouted, and then laughed. "I fooled them—fooled them all— I pretended—every day I pretended and smiled at them all, and they never caught on. They still haven't caught on—they never will. I fooled dumb old Deb too—" She stopped again and frowned, her mood of elation dissipated. Her words were to Jimmy though she kept her eyes on Gretchen. "You think I did? Fooled Deb?"

He shrugged. "So far, maybe, but not for long."

Sheila's lower lip went out in another pout as she stared at Gretchen. "I was fooling everyone—having fun. Then you came along and spoiled it all. You knew."

"But I didn't!" Gretchen heard herself pleading. "I didn't. I didn't really see you that day. To know you, I mean. I didn't recognize you at church—or at your house. I wouldn't have known about—about it. The baby, I mean. I never thought of you when I heard about it. I never would have. I wouldn't have known if you hadn't done this." Her voice fell silent as her eyes begged for their mercy.

Sheila stared back, frowning, trying to follow the meaning of the words. Then she suddenly giggled.

"Did you hear that, Jimmy? Did you hear what she said? We did all this for nothing. She didn't know it was us. We were scaring her for nothing." She giggled again. "It's a good thing we didn't know because then we wouldn't have had all this fun."

Gretchen stared at Sheila as she stood there laughing in the bright sunlight of the clearing. *This is all just a joke to her*, she thought wonderingly, and watched as Sheila slowly raised the gun and aimed at her forehead.

"You want to pray?" Sheila asked suddenly. "You want me to teach you a prayer?"

Gretchen stared at her, at the gun still pointing steadily at her, and realized that Sheila was perfectly serious.

"There's time, you know," Sheila repeated. "We're not in that much of a rush. I can wait if you want to pray."

Gretchen's hands clawed at the trunk of the tree behind her. The girl was mad. There was no hope of escaping from her.

SEVEN

IN THAT INSTANT while Sheila stood waiting with the deadly weapon held so casually ready, and Jimmy stood idly watching, and Gretchen pleaded silently, frantically, *O God, please help me! please save me!* a bird scolded suddenly in a tree at the edge of the clearing, and at the sharp interruption Sheila's gaze jerked away from Gretchen momentarily.

In that second a rope whirled out of nowhere, pinioning Sheila's arms. As her arms were yanked to her sides, the gun flew out of her hand and across the clearing into the underbrush, where a shot exploded harmlessly into the ground. Jimmy made a dive for the gun. But, as he did, a figure in blue catapulted from the bushes at the edge of the clearing and tackled him. Another figure raced past Gretchen's blurred vision to fall on Jimmy, and she heard the sharp click of handcuffs.

Gretchen felt her knees sagging as David's arms caught her up and held her tightly, smoothing her tangled hair back and murmuring her name over and over with words coming from a great distance, "Thank You, God! Thank You! Thank You!"

From the safety of his arms but still trembling, she

watched as Sheila and Jimmy were pulled to their feet, both of them mouthing obscenities. They struggled and kicked at the other policeman who had joined Jack. Sheila was not in handcuffs, but the lasso still circled her as a policeman on either side held her firmly and another gripped Jimmy's arm. They were finally walked off down the narrow path, and Gretchen, watching, heard David say something about police cars following them and parking at the edge of the forest preserve to avoid attracting Jimmy's attention.

"You saw—you heard?"

David nodded, his cheek against her hair.

Gretchen looked then at Jack, who hadn't gone with the other policemen, and from him to Debra, who stood off to one side of the clearing, a pitiful, shaken figure. Gretchen reached up to David's face, holding it between her trembling hands.

"Oh, David, I was sure—so sure I'd never see you again—David, they were so awful! Sheila— You wouldn't believe—you'll never know how she was! She said terrible things. She looked so different—so evil—"

The long, shuddering sobs came then; and David let her cry out her release from terror, holding her tenderly and patting her and smoothing her hair and kissing her eyes and cheeks and lips.

Finally she was quiet, and he gave her his handkerchief. Then she could begin to think and ask questions.

"But how did you find me? How did you know where I was or who I was with? You couldn't have suspected Sheila. If only I had stayed in the house the way you told me to!" And then again, "How did you know where to look for me? Did someone see the license number?" She looked from him to Debra. *How much was she in on this?* she wondered silently.

David led her over to a grassy embankment in the full sunlight. "Here, sit down and lean against me." He helped her ease her tired body to the ground and then turned. "Debra, come over and sit down too."

She shook her head and turned away, her arm against a tree, hiding her face. David motioned to Jack, who went over and took her arm gently, turning her around and talking to her quietly. She came then without resisting and sat down facing them, avoiding Gretchen's eyes.

David said quietly, "Now tell us all you know, Debra."

Her hands plucked nervously at tufts of grass as she kept her face averted.

"Tell us, Debra," he repeated gently. "Don't blame yourself for what happened. You can't help what they did. Remember, you're the one who saved her. If it weren't for you, we never would have known where to look. We would never have gotten here in time." As he spoke he reached to put his arm around Gretchen, and she clung to him.

Debra gave her a quick glance from under lowered lids and swallowed painfully as she began to talk in a low, halting voice, so faint that Gretchen had to lean forward to hear her.

"I guess it all really started when we were in eighth grade. Sheila wanted so much to be in with the popu-

163

lar crowd. And because she was pretty and friendly and really *nice*—then—everybody liked her. She could smile at people and talk so easily and be so much fun and was really—*nice.*" She stressed the word, begging them to understand.

"So she was in things—the school plays and stuff—and she had dates, lots of them, just mostly doing fun things after school and goofing around. At first she dated guys from church. But then—after a while—" Debra's words were dragging now, "after a while it seemed like being popular with kids was more important than anything else. She got so she hated to go to church because the kids she was going around with didn't. But she went. Because Mom and Dad expected her to. They just took for granted we wanted to go because we always had when we were little. And we did want to. And Sheila did—at first. But then she didn't want to, but she didn't let on."

Her voice stopped, and then she burst out, "I think if just once Sheila could have said right out, 'Do I have to go?' or 'I don't want to go to church this time,' or 'Why do we always go to church?' it might have—have helped. But Mom and Dad just always acted so—well, smug about it. You know, the 'Of course our girls go to church even if other kids don't, and so of course our girls wouldn't do anything wrong.' I'm not blaming them," she added hastily. "They're just great. But they wouldn't have understood how Sheila felt. They wouldn't have *understood!*

"The trouble was—" And now enormous round tears were rolling down Debra's cheeks and running off her chin. "The trouble was Sh-Sheila had begun to do wrong things. Way last year. And—I—I—it's partly my f-fault because when I c-could have to-told s-someone when there was s-still t-time, I didn't and then it was t-too late. Because then she f-fell for Jimmy. I mean, she *really* f-fell for him."

So Debra wasn't jealous of Sheila for having Jimmy, Gretchen thought. *Then she must have hung around them so much because she was worried about his influence over Sheila.* She listened as Debra went on in a bleak, despairing tone.

"He used drugs, though I don't know how much. Everyone—all the kids, I mean—knew it. And Sheila knew. But she s-said she n-never would." Debra stopped to wipe at the tears and swallowed her sobs. "And I don't think she did, at least not very much. But everything Jimmy told her to do, she did, no matter what. It was like she was under his spell and she *wanted* to be.

"Dad and Mom didn't like him, though I don't think they knew exactly why. He could pretend to be very nice to adults," she added in a hard tone of scorn. "But inside he was just terrible! Mom and Dad hated to tell Sheila she couldn't go with him because they thought she might be a good influence on him. Jimmy pretended at first that he went to church. Not ours but another. But when Dad found out he didn't, he told Sheila she couldn't date him regularly. And Sheila pretended she didn't mind not dating him. She said she'd only see him once in a while. She claimed she wanted to get him started coming to church. And they believed her. Sheila was always good at covering up.

165

She could smile at you, and you wouldn't know how horrible she was inside."

Gretchen closed her eyes and shuddered. "I know," she whispered. "I know!"

"I didn't know about the little boy!" Debra burst out then. "I was afraid they had done something, but I didn't know what. I didn't know it would be something so terrible! Sheila is my sister—my *twin*—and I couldn't tell on her for some things. I just couldn't. But I would have told if I had known about the little boy. Really I would have!"

She looked from one to the other, begging to be believed, and David said gently, "I'm sure you would have. You wouldn't have covered even for your sister for something that terrible."

Debra turned then and looked directly at Gretchen. "That's why I came with Sheila to your house that night even when I hadn't been invited and Mom thought it wasn't nice of me to barge in. She didn't understand why I insisted on going, and I couldn't tell her. I didn't know how to tell her. There wasn't anything that I could say for sure was wrong. But I was sure Jimmy and Sheila were planning something, and I didn't want Sheila to be there with you alone. I didn't think they would really *do* anything. I mean—I—I thought they would probably just play a joke on you, but I was sure it would be something mean that would scare you. Like they did the night before in the bushes. When I heard about it, I knew Jimmy had done it. Sheila was home in bed, but I was sure she was in on the plans."

She was silent for a moment and then finished

miserably, "Mom thought I was jealous of Sheila and wanted to follow her everywhere because I—I liked Jimmy." She shuddered. "I hated him! I was afraid of him. I had to follow them all I could, and I couldn't explain why. And I didn't dare let Sheila know I suspected anything. Even about the wire that morning—even though she pretended to be so worried about you. I knew it was all fake except for her feeling sick when she saw you were bleeding."

And that was fake too, Gretchen thought, but didn't say it to Debra.

"If you had only told your parents," Jack spoke for the first time. "Why didn't you tell them?"

Debra went white at the accusation in his voice. "They would never have believed me," she whispered in defense. Then she put her face in her hands. "They won't believe it now."

David stood up and helped Gretchen to her feet. "We'll have to try," he said.

They followed him along the narrow path back toward the main road. Off in the distance Gretchen could hear children's voices squealing with laughter, and her hand tightened in David's. How nearly she had come to never hearing sounds like that again. It was unbelievable even yet that she was safe and walking with David back along the path down which she had stumbled a brief, endless hour ago with Sheila's gun in her back and fear in her throat.

Then she realized that David hadn't answered her most important question. She asked it again.

"But I still don't understand how you found me. I didn't think anyone was outside to see the car."

"You can thank Debra," David answered briefly.

"But she wasn't there. No one was. Not even the car at first," she protested, and closed her eyes against the memory of the convertible sliding quietly to the curb, with Sheila sitting in it and smiling at her.

David was explaining. "Debra knew that Sheila was meeting Jimmy someplace this morning. She followed them on her bike and was sure something was up when she found they were heading in our direction. They were a long way ahead of her, of course, but they must have cruised around the block a number of times trying to decide how to—get you." He stopped, his mouth grim. "Debra stopped around the corner where she could watch without being seen. Then you came out, and after a minute the car pulled up beside you. She saw you talking to them and saw you get in the car and it looked so natural, as though you got in because you wanted to. But something made her afraid—"

"It was partly the way Sheila was dressed," Debra interrupted in a thin voice. "She never wore clothes like that around the house. I knew she had them, but she said they were for a beach party she went to once. Mom and Dad don't mind slacks and stuff, but they don't like us to wear this freaky, way-out stuff. So after they had turned the corner out of sight, I rode over to where the car had been, and I saw the envelope on the ground—"

"My letter!" Gretchen exclaimed. "I forgot about it."

"I knew something was wrong, or you wouldn't

have dropped it and not noticed it. You would have picked it up."

David picked up the story. "So Debra decided she had to do something, and she remembered that you had said once that there was a policeman living on your block."

"That's another thing," Debra broke in again. "When we came over to return your lipstick that time, there was a policeman at your house."

"That's when I took care of Brian." Gretchen looked at Debra as she tried to remember the scene. "But— but you came after he had gone. I remember because I was picking some flowers for Brian when your car stopped. And he had gone by then."

Debra shook her head. "No, he was there. We saw him. Only Sheila drove around the block a couple of times until he left." She looked her question. "Why was he there?"

Gretchen explained, and Debra shook her head again. "We didn't know then that he was a neighbor. And I didn't know that Sheila was scared when she saw you talking to him. She must have thought you were telling him about seeing the car. That must be why they started the phone calls. I think—I hope—at first they only intended to scare you away. But then they sort of got carried away with their plans. I think it must have seemed like a—a game to them," she finished with a note of wonder and disbelief.

Gretchen got into the car as Jack held the door open, and sat close to David, remembering Sheila's excited giggle as she had talked about having fun. She half turned then to look at Debra in the back seat. "But this

169

morning? How did you know which neighbor was the policeman? Which house to go to?"

"She didn't," David answered. "But Ruth came home just at that minute. She'd taken Brian to the drugstore. Debra asked who the policeman was, and Ruth called Jack right away. They put out an immediate all-alert bulletin, and someone spotted the car just before it turned off the road into the forest preserve entrance. If they hadn't—" He stopped, his voice breaking.

And Jack said, "We wouldn't have thought to come here. The place had been under surveillance, but that was lifted a few days ago. We would have had no reason to connect this with that murder. They would have been successful again if Debra hadn't seen them in time, and if we hadn't gotten here right away."

"Apparently I got home just after they picked you up," David went on. "Debra was standing in front of the house and ran to the car. Jack pulled up in the squad car just then, and we followed him. He kept in touch with the other cars so we knew where to go."

There was a question she had to ask. "When—when did they—when I saw them in the car that day, was the little boy—" She couldn't finish.

"Yes," David answered gravely. "They had kept him there in the forest preserve from the time they took him. They fed him at first. I don't know whether or not they originally intended to—do what they did. When you saw them they were on their way to swim after—after they had finished."

"The milk bottle," Gretchen said. "The baby bottle—it was in the box on the back seat. I saw it and didn't understand what it meant—didn't think it had any significance."

"She said—the girl said—they threw it into the water when they went to the beach. The police are probably there now looking for it," Jack answered. "She laughed," he said wonderingly. "She laughed. She thought it was funny."

There was a strangled sound from the back seat. "I c-c-can't t-tell my p-parents. I just can't. They thought Sheila was so p-p-perfect."

David glanced back at her in the rearview mirror, his face shadowed with sympathy. "I called your minister those few minutes we stopped at the police station. I told him what we suspected. He said he would go right over."

They drove in silence the rest of the way to the Carlson home. Debra sat for a moment looking toward the closed front door.

"Where have they taken her?" she asked finally.

Jack cleared his throat. "To the police station. They have to get a statement from them."

"Will they keep them there? Sheila too? Will they have to go to—jail?" Her voice cracked on the last word and she clenched her teeth together.

Jack waited a moment. Then because there seemed to be no way to say it gently, he answered, "Yes, until the trial."

Gretchen looked with Debra at the spacious house, now with a shuttered, closed-in air, and wondered what was going on behind the filmy curtains in the once sunny room where there had never until now been tragedy.

"That's the minister's car in the driveway," Debra said. "I'm glad he's here first." She got out then, and they watched as she went up the walk slowly, opened the door, and closed it without a backward look.

There were so many other questions Gretchen wanted to ask, so many details that weren't clear, but she was too exhausted to think them through now. She leaned her head back against the car seat as David drove home; and listened as he said over his shoulder to Jack, "Thank Ruth for me. It was her quickness in getting the call through to the station that got the first squad car to the forest preserve in time to see them turn in."

"She really did it, didn't she?" Jack's voice was proud.

"I hope it won't worry her," Gretchen said. "I mean, the fact that real danger was so close to her."

"No, I think it will help her. She has been so worried over just the *thought* of danger, that having faced it close at hand and come through it will make her braver. But you should have told us," he scolded her gently, "about the scare that night. And the wire. Maybe we could have forestalled this today."

Then he shook his head. "No, you had no idea who was doing it, and I don't think there's a chance that we would have connected your disappearance with the little boy's kidnapping. There would have been nothing to tie them together—no similarities at all. Even Debra's suspicions—provided she had spoken up—wouldn't have been enough evidence to connect the two events."

"Did you have any clues at all in the kidnapping?" David asked.

"Not really," Jack admitted. "We thought possibly a woman was involved. We found a footprint that was small and narrow, more like a woman's than a man's. But who would have connected a terrible thing like that with a girl like Sheila? You know—pretty, smiling girl; good family; wealthy, church-going people."

Gretchen listened wearily as he talked, aware of how tired she was, but bothered by this question that needed an answer more than all the others. This business of Sheila and church. *If Sheila really believed what her mother said she did, then how could she be the way I saw her?* she wondered. She shook the thoughts away. This would have to be explored carefully, for it was a fragile thing. Too much depended on the answer—the Carlsons' belief in God, David's interest in the Bible, her own inexplicable cry to God for help. There was a time, she knew, when she would have dismissed her frantic prayer with a scornful "Everyone begs God for help when he's in a tight spot. It's a superstitious hangover from a primitive culture. Like a rabbit's foot or the good-luck charm some people carry."

But it had been more than that with her back there in the clearing an hour ago. There hadn't been anyone else to turn to, that was true. But she had to admit —but only to herself—that even if there had been, she would have called on God. For somehow she had known instinctively that there was more than her physical safety at stake. If she had lost her life back there, she would have lost far more. It was all tied in

173

with the minister's square. One thing she was sure of. Her once-confident words to Mrs. Carlson about being strong enough to take trouble without outside help were not true.

She opened her eyes as David stopped the car in the driveway. Jack got out and leaned down to look in at them. "After a while—tomorrow, maybe—we'll have to ask you to come down to the station and make an identification—"

Gretchen cringed. "I can't! I can't face them! Do I have to?" she pleaded. "You saw—you all heard—"

He nodded. "But we'll need a statement from you, too. It won't take long. And maybe you won't have to see them. But don't worry. Try not to think about it. They can't hurt you or frighten you anymore." He shook his head in pity. "It's their parents, their families, they are hurting now. But I don't suppose they care about that, or they wouldn't have done this in the first place." He shook his head again. "It's unbelievable that they shouldn't have suspected."

Gretchen stared somberly out of the car, watching Jack stride away and thinking again of the lovely sunlit house where this horrible thing had entered unexpectedly. And the question in her mind was insistent. *Was God still real to them?*

She let David help her out of the car and up the walk. It was strange to go into the house and not feel a compulsion to bolt the door behind her—to know that the fear and worry were lifted. It seemed incredible that the neighborhood was unchanged, that not even the people in the houses on either side knew of the tragedy that had been so narrowly averted for her. She stood in the living room and looked around gratefully

174

at the dear familiarity she had left so thoughtlessly and to which she might never have returned, and she felt her eyes blinded by tears of relief and gratitude that she had been rescued.

"I can't believe I'm really here," she said wonderingly. "That I'm safe! I can't believe it! When I stood by the car and saw the gun—when I looked down at Sheila's face so much the same and yet so different—when I saw it and knew what she was like—oh, David, if you had seen her! If you had seen the look on her face!"

David tightened his hold on her, and she leaned against him, crying again weakly in relief and wondering if she would ever really forget those long moments of terror.

She jerked in alarm at the sound of someone at the door and David quieted her with a gentle "Easy now. There's nothing to be worried about anymore."

As he went toward the door, they heard Ruth call, "Gretchen? David? Is it all right if I come in?"

David held the door open, and Ruth came in with a rush and flung her arms around Gretchen, hugging her.

"Oh, Gretchen, I couldn't *believe* it when Jack came home just now and said you'd been found and everything was OK because I was sure they would never find the car and make it in time, and I told Jack it was the first time I ever knew that prayer did some good, because you'll never *believe* how I prayed for you after that girl came and I had called Jack and then everybody went; and the only thing I could do to help was stay home with Brian like always, only this time I *really* prayed. You'll never believe how I prayed."

Gretchen listened, and out of the jumble of emotions that filled her—amusement at Ruth's usual rush of words, weariness at their unending flow, appreciation for her concern—only one thought really surfaced intelligibly, and that was to wonder to whom Ruth had prayed since she didn't believe in God.

But she answered gratefully, "Thanks for acting so quickly without waiting to ask Debra a lot of questions. If you hadn't—well, I might not be sitting here now," she finished shakily.

Ruth sat pleating and unpleating the edge of her skirt and feeling for words which poured out again.

"I just feel *terrible* that you were going through all this and all the time you just let me rattle on about all my imaginary problems instead of telling me about your real ones and letting me help—at least I think I would have helped. I would have tried to, anyway, though of course I should have been a good enough friend to have noticed that something was wrong. And I told Jack when he came home and said you were safe that I was going to stop being such a drag on other people and especially on him and try to be a better neighbor."

"I know," Gretchen nodded, remembering that she had had those same thoughts about Ruth—when was it? Just this morning, though it seemed eons ago now. Ruth stood up. "I've got to run, because Jack stayed with Brian so I could come over, but he has to get back on duty. I'm not going to ask you anything about it now since Jack has told me some of it, and he said not

176

to bother you with a lot of questions. But when you feel like talking, *if* you feel like talking about it, I'd like to know especially how teenagers, kids that young, *church* kids, could do such terrible things." She went out shaking her head.

This was part of the question that nagged at Gretchen, but only a part. There was another one that lay hidden like an iceberg, an under-the-surface question of why Sheila had done it. Sheila—with all she had of things to make her happy. And if things weren't enough, she'd had love too, she'd been surrounded by love all her life at home, from her parents. And if that love were not enough, Sheila had had God too.

And this was the question that lay beneath all the others. Did that mean that God hadn't been enough either? And if that were true for Sheila, would it be true for someone else also? Could you really count on God to be—what were those words David had said once?—a refuge and strength, a very present help in trouble? He hadn't been for Sheila.

But a faint memory worried at her, and she frowned over it, trying to trace it back through the maze of events and conversations. There was something— yes, the night the girls had stayed with her. She had asked Sheila a direct question about her faith, and Sheila had— She hadn't answered! Gretchen caught her breath as she remembered how skillfully Sheila had shifted the burden of answering to Debra, and she hadn't noticed it at the time.

She was aware then that David was watching her intently and she smiled back at him. She gave up trying to find answers to the puzzling questions and was content to sit under the shade of a tree the rest of the afternoon. David suggested having a cold supper, and she helped prepare a salad plate and butter rolls. He put a record on the stereo, and they carried their plates into the living room and ate without talking.

When they finished, David asked, "You want your favorite comedy?" and moved toward the TV. But Gretchen caught at his hand, stopping him. She looked up at him through eyes suddenly filling again with tears, though she tried to check them.

"Not tonight, David. I can't laugh tonight. I keep thinking about—about—"

"Try not to," he urged. "Try to forget. It's all over now. They can't do anything more to you."

"No, not that. I'm not thinking of that. It's them —the Carlsons and Debra. Yes, I'm thinking of Sheila too, but I can't feel sorry for her. I should perhaps, but she was so horrible. She *knew* what she was doing —she wanted to do it—she was enjoying it." She broke off to shiver again. "But it's her parents I feel sorry for. What must they be feeling—thinking— doing?"

David got up then to walk restlessly around the room, and her eyes followed him, noting his agitation.

"What's the matter? Is there something you aren't telling me?" she asked in quick alarm.

He shook his head. "No. No—it's just that there's so much at stake!" The words burst from him as he went to stand by the front door, looking out into the gathering darkness.

She looked at his back, not understanding what was causing the desperation in him, but feeling it in the urgency of his voice.

"What do you mean?"

He turned then to look at her from across the room and came slowly back to sit down beside her. She looked at his troubled profile as he frowned down at his fingers laced tightly together.

Finally he said in a low voice as though he were talking to himself, "So much depends on them. On whether what they said they believed is still real to them in the face of this."

"The Carlsons?"

He nodded without looking at her. Then he went on, "You know that story in the Bible I told you about? The one where Daniel prayed to his God even when it was dangerous to do it? Well, there's another one something like it in the same book. It's about three of Daniel's friends who were going to be burned alive because of their belief in God. And they said their God was powerful enough to deliver them, but even if He didn't, even if He let them be burned up, they were still going to believe in Him, they would still trust Him."

She thought about it. "And you wonder if the Carlsons will be able to say that now in spite of Sheila?"

He nodded.

"And if they can't? Will it make a difference to you? To what you believe?"

"I—don't—know."

His words were spaced evenly, deliberately, but

there was a cry in them, and she frowned, concentrating on something, some inconsistency in what he was saying.

"Were those men you were talking about—the ones in the story—were they saved?"

"Yes. But first they were thrown in the furnace. And then God took them out of it, and they weren't hurt."

"Oh."

It was all so strange, so unreal to her that she couldn't put it all together. She knew that at another time she would have laughed at the impossible story. But she couldn't laugh at miracles today, for she had lived through one. She looked lovingly at David. Her crisis was over and she was safe, but he was still going through a crisis. She watched him as he sat despondent, his shoulders hunched, and ached to help him. But she had no words to use, no understanding to give. Then he straightened and looked at her, a smile deepening the lines around his mouth but lifting the shadows from his face.

"I should be the happiest man in the world to have you home and safe," he exclaimed. "When I came back this morning to find you gone and heard Debra's story—"

She heard the break in his voice and looked up at him penitently. "I know now that I never should have left the house. You told me not to. But the mailbox looked so close and I was so restless, I felt so penned in. I never thought anything could happen. If only I had stayed home!"

He shook his head positively. "No. If you hadn't

gone and they hadn't picked you up, you would still be in danger. They had gone so far in their plans that they couldn't turn back. They were determined to get rid of you some way, somehow. Now at least it's over. You are safe, and they won't be able to harm someone else."

"It's over for us."

She felt his chin brush against her hair as he nodded. "For us, yes. But not for Sheila. And not for them. Poor Debra," he finished softly. "What a burden she must be carrying, wondering if it would have made a difference if she had voiced her suspicions."

Gretchen's thoughts were suddenly clear, and she spoke quickly before they could slip away.

"You know, David, I don't quite know how to say this because I haven't been reading the Bible, or—or even listening to the minister when we went to church. But if you believe in God, don't you believe in Him no matter what? I mean, no matter what other people say or think or do? Isn't He God regardless of what happens? If He *is* God, I mean?"

She looked at him anxiously, afraid she had said the wrong thing, for he sat motionless. Then he looked at her and a smile broke over his face.

"Of course! Of course, you're right. That's what they were saying, wasn't it? Those young men in the Bible. They believed *God*, and it didn't matter what He let happen to them."

He was so exultant that she looked at him wistfully, wondering if some of that would ever come to her.

"But that doesn't mean that what the Carlsons are going through isn't important," she said anxiously. "I mean, we still should care about them and their suffering and how they are going to take all of this sorrow."

"Yes, we must care. I do care. But in spite of that, how they take their tragedy can't change what I believe. I have to believe in God without depending on other people's experiences or someone else's faith." He looked at her and said humbly, "Darling, thank you for showing me that. Can you accept it too?"

She shook her head. "No. I can't. I just can't believe that easily."

They looked at each other gravely, and in the silence that stretched between them, a car door slammed shut, and they could hear footsteps on the sidewalk. David went to the open door, and Gretchen listened to his warm voice as he said, "Come in," and held the screen door open.

Gretchen watched as the Carlsons stepped hesitantly inside and stood in the doorway, looking at her. His face was haggard, her eyes bloodshot and swollen from tears.

"We had to come," he said simply and stood waiting.

David put out his hand and grasped Mr. Carlson's. "Sit down, Eric," he said, his own voice husky.

"We didn't know if you would ever want to see us again, but we had to see you," Mrs. Carlson said in a low, heavy voice. "We had to tell you how sorry we are for what our daughter has done to you and how we thank God that you are safe."

Gretchen felt herself crumbling inside. She hadn't known what reaction to expect from them. Shock, of course. But anger, perhaps? Recrimination? Indignation at Sheila for the shame and disgrace she had brought them? There was none of that. Only sorrow and bewilderment and the loving words, *our daughter*.

"Needless to say," Mr. Carlson continued, "we had no idea what was going on. It seems incredible that we shouldn't have known, shouldn't have suspected *something*. But we didn't. All the cases I've seen in court—all the young people from good homes I've seen go wrong—knowing it could happen in any family—nothing prepared me for my own child!" His hands were gripped together so hard the knuckles were white. "Sheila was always so frank, so responsive, so *loving* a child, we thought." He looked helplessly at his wife for confirmation.

"It's been a double blow," she said, her voice a wisp of sound. "First to find that Sheila was—was—like this." Her voice trembled and she stopped to try to hold back tears that came anyway. "I'm sorry," she whispered, wiping futilely at them. "I thought I was all cried out—that there weren't any tears left."

"There will always be tears," her husband said and put his arm protectively around her. He looked at them somberly. "Like other parents we've heard about, read about, who've gone through something like this, we couldn't believe it when Mr. Gorman came this morning. Our Sheila whom we've loved and protected and prayed for—" He bit his lip, and Gretchen felt the tears sliding down her cheeks as she watched them run down his face.

"What did we do wrong?" he asked. "How could

183

this happen? Debra said Sheila rebelled against being made to go to church. Did we *make* her?" He looked at his wife's bowed head. "We went *together*. She—we thought she liked it. She said she believed in Jesus. Did she? Was it all pretense? Did the Bible verses and the prayers mean nothing to her? Do *we* mean nothing to her? She wouldn't see us this afternoon when we went down. She said she didn't want to."

The pain was sharp in his voice, and they could only sit in helpless silence in the face of his deep grief.

Mrs. Carlson looked at Gretchen and then away again quickly, twisting a handkerchief between her shaking fingers. Her voice was still trembling, and she tried to steady it.

"The other thing that makes this so hard is that she did this to you. I keep thinking about our conversations—about the questions you asked me and the confident answers I gave. I was so sure of our girls. And all the time this was going on." She stopped again to steady her voice, and Gretchen ached as she saw her anguish. "I've been thinking about you. I've been so afraid this will turn you away. How can you believe—after this? How can you be sure God will help you after this? How can you be sure God will help you after seeing this?"

"Because it isn't God who failed, Gudrun. You and I failed. Sheila failed. God didn't." Mr. Carlson's voice was almost a stern rebuke, and Gretchen held her breath as she watched Mrs. Carlson nod in agreement, the tears falling in big splashes on her crumpled handkerchief. She looked up at him, and the two of them might have been alone—so intent were they on each other.

"We know that, but do they?" She gestured at Gretchen and David without looking at them. "What if this keeps them from coming to God? It could, you know."

"They have to believe God for themselves," he argued back. "If they believed only because of us, because of what *we* said or did, it wouldn't last. Something else could come along and sweep their faith away. It's got to be based on God—no matter what."

David spoke then, and Gretchen listened to his quiet voice saying the words she had known were there waiting to be said. "Don't worry about—" He hesitated for a moment and then finished, "Don't worry about us." She could feel the quick appealing glance he gave her, but she didn't look up from her hands gripped tightly together in her lap.

She listened as he went on, "What you've already shown us of your faith is more important than anything else. My wife has already said what you just said, Eric." Gretchen lifted her head and saw the pride shining in David's eyes as he looked back at her. "She said it too—that God is God regardless of what happens. What you've said here tonight proves that. That you can think of us in spite of all you are going through—well, it's just another confirmation that what you believe is real. Don't worry about us." He smiled at them confidently.

Mr. Carlson stood up, drawing his wife to her feet and supporting her tenderly with his arm. "I'm glad," he answered simply. "We've been concerned about you all day." Then he looked at them sadly. "We have great restitution to make to you for our daughter. We can't take away the fright and anguish you went through because of her, but we are responsible for her actions as much now as we always have been. The police—" He stopped and swallowed, his jaw muscles tight. "The police will want you to come down tomorrow and prefer charges."

David shook his head quickly. "There are no charges. We will have to state what happened, of course. But Gretchen is safe, nothing happened to her, and that is all that matters."

"Thank you. You are very generous." Mrs. Carlson spoke through trembling lips. "There is another matter of course—so much worse. We—we are on our way now to see the little boy's family—to see what we can do—" She broke off, crying again.

"Mr. Gorman is going with us. We need his help in facing them."

Gretchen watched as David let them out the door and then asked, "What will happen to Sheila?"

He shook his head. "It was murder, and they will have to take the consequences. She admits to being as guilty as Jimmy, so she will have to share the punishment. There will be a trial, I suppose, though I don't know how they handle juvenile cases. One thing is sure. It's going to be a long, hard time ahead for the Carlsons."

Gretchen turned and wandered through the house, straightening a fold of a curtain, shifting the position of a figurine on the bookshelf, wiping a bit of dust from the stereo, pinching a dead leaf from a plant. They were familiar gestures, done, she knew, in an attempt to bring back the normalcy of the life they'd known before David had gone to church. But that couldn't be. That life would never return, because David had changed. And she had been confronted by God. Her independence and self-sufficiency had not been enough in a crisis.

The question had to be answered. Why had she cried out to God when death stared at her? Was it only instinct? Just desperation because she thought no human help was near? Or was it a deep, heartfelt yearning for God that had been aroused by the words from David's Bible? There were those other words:

> He comes to thee all unaware
> And makes thee own His loving care.

The words and melody of the song had haunted her since yesterday, and now she had found them true. She *had* experienced God's loving care.

At last she said, "I guess those things are true."

"What things?"

"What you've been saying from the Bible. About God." She shook her head. "But I don't understand. God is a refuge and help to the Carlsons even now, but He isn't to Sheila. He rescued me, but He let the little boy die." She frowned at the contradictions.

Then she looked across at David as he stood watching her. He had moved from unbelief to faith so easily. From uncertainty and doubt to assurance, from a world of shadowed fears to one of shining light.

"David," she said uncertainly. Then with more

confidence, "David, I want to be able to say those words—'Where thou goest, I will go, thy God shall be my God'—but I don't know how. I need help."

His face lighted, and he came toward her, pulling the Bible from his pocket. "Here it is," he said, the marked and underlined pages falling open. "This is the Book that tells about God. We'll read it together and find the answers."

Moody Press, a ministry of the Moody Bible Institute, is designed for education, evangelization and edification. If we may assist you in knowing more about Christ and the Christian life, please write us without obligation to: Moody Press, c/o MLM, Chicago, Illinois 60610.